AF243734

CAFFEINATED OWL PRESS · 2012

THE BOYFRIEND EXPERIENCE

ALEXIS E. SKYE

The Boyfriend Experience

Cover and book design by A. D. Cooper

This is an original work of fiction. Any similarity to actual persons, alive or dead, or real events is purely coincidental and unintentional. The material found herein contains graphical depictions of sexually explicit situations and is intended for mature audiences only.

ISBN: 978-0-9880183-1-0
eBook ISBN: 978-0-9880183-0-3

Caffeinated Owl Press
www.caffeinatedowl.com

*For B
Without your encouragement I wouldn't
have made it this far.*

*And E & L
For all of your "inspirations" and being
there to lend some helping hands.*

THE BOYFRIEND EXPERIENCE

THE FAINT BUT insistent buzzing woke him. It took him a few seconds blinking his eyes to realize it was his phone, vibrating against the smooth bedside table. He tried reaching for it, but the hairy, muscular arm slung over his waist pulled him back against a solid wall of muscle.

"Ethan?" The owner of the arm muttered in a raspy voice against the nape of his neck, barely awake.

"Ssh…" Ethan moved the arm gently from his waist before reaching back to peck a kiss against the man's temple. "Just my phone."

Sliding off the bed, Ethan picked up the buzzing phone and padded out of the bedroom, still naked. The sun was already up, and it cast a faint golden glow over the granite counters in the open-concept kitchen.

"What?" he answered the phone harshly as he looked around for his forgotten briefs from last night.

"This is your morning call, sleepyhead."

"It's eight in the morning on a Saturday, you jackass," Ethan complained in a muted yell; Darcy had a terrible sense of timing.

"Eight in the morning is when normal people get up, Ethan," Darcy said. "And why are you whispering?"

"Because John is still sleeping and I'm trying not to wake him? And since when are *we* ever considered *normal* people?" Ethan said as he looked under the black leather sectional. "Aha!"

"You stayed the night?" Darcy's voice raised an octave. "That was not part of the arrangement!"

"Dude, chill. He said he'd pay; said he wanted to make me breakfast, so I said sure, why not." Ethan rolled his eyes. "Darcy, you're my agent, not my mother. And remember to add the extra time to the final invoice."

"Jesus Christ, Ethan."

"Hey, it's my charm, what can I say? Plus, you're getting a cut of that so stop your whining." Ethan held the phone between his ear and his shoulder, awkwardly trying to pull on his shorts. "You still haven't gotten to the part where you explain why you're calling me at eight in the morning on a Saturday."

"I've got a new client here that fits your specialty," Darcy paused. Ethan could tell by his hollow sounding voice that he was looking for the file. "Here. Darren Chase. Ever heard of him?"

"Can't say I have. Should I?"

"Well, he's got quite a resume here. Hmm…" Darcy paused again. "You know what, call me when you're home. I'll email you his file so you can have a look before you decide."

"Okie dokie. Bye." Ethan hung up without waiting for a reply.

He plopped down on the sectional and let the soft leather take his weight, burying his face into his hand as he tilted his head back. He was wide-awake now after that phone call and there was no way he'd be able to go back to bed. "Damn you, Darcy," he growled into his hand.

Rubbing his face a couple of times, he stuffed his phone into his coat that hung by the door and decided to go check on the man in the bedroom.

He padded back towards the bed, keeping his footsteps as light as possible. The man wrapped an arm around his waist when he sat down at the edge of the mattress.

"Morning," the man said, his voice muffled by the pillow.

"G'morning, John." Ethan smiled, leaning down to give the man a kiss. "Didn't mean to awake you this early."

"Hmm… it's okay but you'll have to make it up to me." John rolled onto his back, pulling Ethan down to lie on top of him. "Who was that?"

"Just work." Ethan nuzzled against the firm, muscular chest of the man underneath. "You know, I remember someone saying he's going to make me breakfast."

"Oh, really?" John tapped his chin. "I guess I did, didn't I?"

"Or do you want me to make it instead? Breakfast in bed?" Ethan's lips pulled into a smirk as he rested his chin on John's chest. "You can sleep for a bit more while I get to work."

"No, I promised you, and a man must keep his promises." John pulled Ethan into a kiss before sitting up. "Go get cleaned up. I'll be in the kitchen."

"You sure you don't wanna join me?" Ethan arched an eyebrow as he climbed off the bed.

John snorted a laugh. "You're impossible."

"I know." Ethan grinned, giving the man a wink as he sauntered into the ensuite, closing the door behind him but not locking it.

He adjusted the temperature before stepping into the shower. The hot spray steamed up the bathroom quickly despite its spacious size. Dropping his head, Ethan let his mind wander as the water poured over his lanky frame.

The door opened and a pair of hands rested over his shoulder, massaging lightly before trailing down to his sides then his abs. He leaned his head back as John pulled him flush against his solid body.

"Mmm…" Ethan moaned as John's hands traveled south, palming his early morning erection. He tilted his head slightly to the side to give John more access to his neck as he pressed his ass to the other man's stiff length. "You know, if it were anyone else I'd be charging extra for this. You're lucky I like you a lot," Ethan chuckled as John nibbled and licked his way up Ethan's neck.

"I know," John hummed against the spot behind Ethan's left ear, causing a small gasp of pleasure to escape Ethan's throat.

He pressed Ethan against the glass wall of the shower, his hands caressing Ethan's back lovingly before moving down to Ethan's ass, pushing his cheeks aside to reveal his tight pucker.

Ethan's chest began to heave as John pushed in, slowly opening him back up. He pushed his hips back, rocking against John and crying out as his actions sent John's hard length deeper into him. John stabbed into his ass, grunting with each thrust.

The initial burn quickly dissipated into pleasure and the powerful thrusts left Ethan weak in the knees. Being pressed against the glass was the only thing keeping him standing up straight.

He reached for his own aching cock and began to stroke himself to the rhythm of John pumping into him. His moans became louder and louder as pleasure built towards his climax.

"I'm coming!"

"Come on, baby," John licked at the sensitive spot behind his ear, nipping at the skin there. "Come for me!"

"Oh god…" Ethan cried out as he streaked the glass wall with his load. He tightened his channel around John's cock as he climaxed.

"Fuck!" John swore, speeding up his erratic thrusts before pulling out and spraying Ethan's back with his warm cream.

John's body was heavy as he draped himself over Ethan. They stayed still like that for a long moment, letting the water wash away the sweat and cum as their chests heaved.

Without a word, Ethan turned in John's arms, reaching for the soap and began washing the man's body. John pecked kisses into Ethan's wet hair as he gently massaged the man's body. After Ethan was done, John pulled him in for a long kiss before stepping out of the shower.

"Soggy bacon and eggs, right?"

Ethan grinned. "Yeah."

Ethan climbed the stairs to his fifth-floor apartment and wondered for the third time in the past five minute why he didn't just move somewhere else that actually had a working elevator. He hated the stairs.

He juggled the bags in one hand as he jiggled the lock open with the other. Once inside, he set the bags on the kitchen counter before taking off his coat and tossing it into the bedroom along with his shoulder bag.

"Damn, it's cold," Ethan muttered to himself as he turned

on the heater. It was the end of November; it wasn't quite winter yet, but it'd started to get uncomfortably cold in his apartment.

After putting the groceries away, he stripped off the polo, sweater and khaki combo and changed into jeans and a long tee. He huffed into his clasped hands before rubbing them to warm up.

He dug his laptop out from the coffee table under a pile of old newspaper and logged in. Frowning at the fifty something new emails of mostly junk, he ticked off the important ones and sent the rest to the trash folder.

The first email was from an online friend of his, emailing him an ebook on neoclassical art that he'd been looking for. He downloaded the book and archived the message. The rest were mostly forwarded messages from Darcy of his clients wanting to know when he'd be available for booking. He decided to look at them later.

The last email contained the file on the new client Darcy told him about that morning. Ethan pursed his lips, as he hovered the pointer over it.

"Ah, fuck it." He'd read it later; he was hungry. He printed the file out and stuffed them into a folder, then went into the kitchen for food.

He cracked open a book that said "The Art of Strategy" on its spine after tossing some frozen leftovers into the microwave. The book was written by a pair of professors from Princeton and Yale and talked about game theory as applied to business and life. It was pretty heavy reading but he devoured it with interest just the same.

In his line of work it paid to be well-read, so he spent every opportunity he had to read up on anything that could come into use.

His phone buzzed as a text came in. It was from John.

Hope you got home okay. Cold outside, take good care of your-self. I'll call after I get back from ATL. Love, J.

Ethan smiled. John was a great guy; one of his favorite clients. He was pushing sixty but he didn't look it at all. A well conditioned body with a full head of hair on top of a handsome face and a sex-drive to match, no one would suspect John to be a day older than fifty. And he was genuinely a nice person, too. Ethan enjoyed spending time with him.

He couldn't help thinking back to what John had said as he was about to leave.

"Ethan," John muttered against his ear, resting his arms over Ethan's shoulders and holding him from behind after Ethan had put on his winter coat. "Stay."

"Stay with me," he'd said. "Please?"

Ethan had smiled but shook his head. Turning around, he'd given John a lingering gentle kiss, cupping the side of his face with a gloved hand. "Have a good time in Atlanta with your family, John."

This wasn't the first time John had asked him to consider something a little more… permanent. It wasn't the first time Ethan had refused the man either.

John was the CFO of a Fortune 500 company but he didn't have the kind of arrogance typical of successful men in New York City, and that made him special. Ethan never minded giving the man extra service but John always insisted on paying him accordingly.

Ethan was what one would refer to as a "professional boy-friend". As a high-end male escort, he provided the experiences of a real-life boyfriend to a very exclusive clientele of rich and famous men. His job was simple: make his clients happy, and make sure no one found out about his existence.

Ethan wasn't his real name either. His real name was Nathaniel de Luca, but everyone called him Nate. Born in New Jersey, Nate had come to the Big Apple with big dreams, only to have his dreams crushed by reality. He worked a bunch of odd jobs here and there before he began working at a club as a go-go boy to make ends meet—and then Darcy had come along and introduced him to the world of escort services.

In another life, he would've loved to explore the possibility of a future with someone like John, if he wasn't a client. And if the man wasn't married with two kids his age.

But he was, on both counts. Too bad.

Plus, Nate wouldn't say he was in love with the man. He was careful not to.

Nate had only one rule when it came to his job: Do not fall in love with the client.

What they did, it was all just an illusion. An illusion of love, built not on trust but on money and the necessity of sex. It wasn't real and Nate was only too aware of that. He'd seen it with others who made the mistake of believing that fantasy. It never ended well.

The microwave beeped. He took his food out and ate as he continued to read.

The red folder with the new client's file sat on the couch next to him, distracting him from his readings. He had to admit, he was curious about the new client, but he wasn't sure if he wanted to take on a new client. In fact, he'd been thinking more and more about how much longer he could do this for a living.

The original plan was to make enough so he could afford to go back to school and finish his degree, but the money was too good. Living in New York City didn't come cheap. He had bills and debts to pay; playing boyfriend ensured that he wouldn't starve and could save some for a rainy day.

Shaking his head, he closed the book and tossed the dishes into the sink to deal with later. Strolling back into the living room, he picked up the red folder and opened it.

The first page of the file contained the basics—name, age, occupation, stats and background. If there was one thing Darcy was good at, it was making sure that the client was clean and worth engaging. There was a picture attached to it. Nate took the page out and stared at the man in the picture.

Darren Chase reminded Nate of Christian Bale a la Bruce Wayne. His hair, dark with a slight wave, was carefully styled to match the expensive suit he wore. The shot was a paper clipping from some business periodical, and the man was smiling at someone or something off to the side. It was really a handsome smile, but the man had a serious, formidable air about him that contrasted strongly with the brilliant smile. The combination sent a shiver down Nate's spine.

Nate pulled his laptop back out and googled Chase's name. There were some news articles about the man's background— graduated MIT with honors, then Harvard Business School, started his company with a fellow classmate from nothing, et cetera. The rest of the more recent articles were from the business section, with speculations of when his company would go public ("maybe sooner than we thought," said one article).

Flipping to the next page of the file, Nate began reading the questionnaire.

"Long-term, full service experience. Need someone who is willing to listen but could carry an intelligent conversation if necessary. Basic cooking skills an asset, but not essential…" Nate read out the long list as he plopped himself back on the couch. The questionnaire the Agency provided the clients was very comprehensive. There was something like five pages of criteria that ranged from domestic skills to sexual practices. "Darcy was right, exactly the kind of client for me."

Darcy's agency wasn't a small one, but there were only a handful of male escorts who serviced male clients and had the necessary skills to pull it off. Nate happened to be one of the best.

He continued reading, then blinked in surprise at the last line. "Willing to pay extra for full-time, 24/7 service. Minimum one month engagement."

Whoa, Nelly!

Full-time services were not unheard of, but it was very rare. Most men Nate had ever engaged were looking for short-term relief on a regular basis—something to take their mind off of the problems in their everyday life, to scratch that itch. All they were looking for was someone who wouldn't judge them to confide in. Very few clients would ever consider hiring someone full time, the main reason being cost.

"No wonder Darcy was so on edge about this," Nate muttered to himself as he set the file down. He needed to think.

He hadn't really given it any thought before today, if he was ever contracted to a full-time engagement. He'd never expected it to come up.

If he were to accept Chase's offer, he'd have to temporarily hand his current clients to someone else while he worked exclusively for this one man. He didn't really like the thought of that. Their business was a competitive one, and there was a very high possibility that he'd lose some of his regulars.

On the other hand, though, if everything went well, he'd have enough money set aside in a few months to retire from the circuit. He'd finally be able to get back to his interrupted life and think about a future.

He let his head drop back against the top of the cushion. He took a deep breath then let it out.

He stared at the ceiling for a long moment before he decided that he wouldn't be able to figure it out sitting in his apartment. He needed some fresh air.

Sitting on a park bench at Pier 11 over-looking the East River at Brooklyn across the water, he took out his phone and dialed Darcy's number from memory. The sun was just about to set and the distant sky beyond Brooklyn looked hazy and dark, as if a storm was about to form.

"Ethan! What's up?" Darcy sounded cheerful, as he always seemed to be. "You read what I sent you yet?"

"I'll take the case," Nate said, pulling his scarf tighter around his neck to block the chill from the brisk wind blowing in from the Atlantic. "Under one condition."

"What kind of condition?"

"Tell Chase I'm willing to commit only if the first date goes well." There would be no point for him to waste his time if they didn't click. "Set it up and email me the details."

"Deal." Nate could hear Darcy's grin across the wire. "You have no idea how much this means to me, man."

Nate rolled his eyes as he disconnected the call. He could hazard a guess—it probably contained a few zeroes.

The lights of the Brooklyn Bridge came on and it looked simply splendid at night, but Nate wasn't in the mood to enjoy the sights. He continued to sit there staring out at the water as the sky darkened, until it was too cold for him.

DARREN CHASE HOOKED a finger under his collar, trying to loosen it a tad as he took a deep breath then let it out in a long sigh. He had all the appearance of a man enjoying a relaxing drink, but he was anything but relaxed.

In fact, he was more nervous than the first time he addressed the media at a company press conference.

The man from the agency, Darcy, had instructed him to pick a place and a time, and told him that someone named "Ethan" would be coming to meet him. He didn't know why he was so nervous. It was supposed to be a simple drink and dinner, maybe some small talk. There was nothing to be nervous about, really.

Well, nothing to be nervous about, except for the fact the man he was meeting was a professional boyfriend—a male escort that provided boyfriend experiences.

They were supposed to go on their first date, at which point Ethan would decide whether to accept his offer of a long term engagement or not. Darren could understand their cautiousness; there was a lot of money and time involved, and he was an unknown to them. He'd done his homework too; the agency he used was one of the most reputable one in New York. It held its clients' satisfaction and protecting its clients' privacy as its number one priority.

He didn't want to seem intoxicated, especially during their first date, but he waved the bartender over and ordered a second drink anyway as he finished his first. Maybe he just needed more liquid courage to get over his nerves.

He'd never seen Ethan—not in person, at least. He'd only seen a picture and it didn't give him much of an impression about what the man really looked like. Then again, he'd never been a very visual person; he was more interested in the interaction and chemistry. Good looks wouldn't hurt though he thought as he anxiously waited.

It didn't really sink in for him until he'd stepped into the restaurant's bar to wait for Ethan, that he was really doing this. He'd never thought about hiring someone who provided this kind of service—it just never occurred to him. Not until an acquaintance of his had brought it up recently when they were chitchatting.

Darren Chase had never had problems attracting sexual attention, whether it was from a man or a woman. He'd hit the jackpot when he started his information technology company with his business partner a dozen years ago, specializing in IT infrastructure and security. He was good-looking, and he had money—a combination that ensured he could have anything and anyone he wanted.

The problem with having money and influence, was that it made it that much harder to find someone who was interested in him as a person, rather than his money. He didn't want just anyone; he wanted a relationship that would last the test of time.

While he'd all but given up on a real relationship, he had his needs. Hiring someone on a long-term basis to provide not only sexual release but also the appearance of a real relationship… it wasn't a bad idea.

"Mr. Chase?" A mild tenor voice roused Darren from his thoughts, and he looked up to find a man in a sharp suit standing next to him with a polite smile. "I'm Ethan. Nice to make your acquaintance."

Darren chuckled at Ethan's words. "You can call me Darren," he said, shaking the young man's out-stretched hand. "And, for the record, formality should be reserved for those you don't like."

"I'll keep that in mind," Ethan said, his smile widened.

"Sit down. What's your poison?" Darren asked, quietly observing Ethan as the man took the seat next to him.

Ethan was only a couple of inches shorter than him, but with a much lankier frame. He had a young looking face—Darren couldn't believe that Ethan was almost thirty years old. He would've guessed that Ethan was still in college if it wasn't for the profile Darcy provided him.

Darren could see why Darcy regarded Ethan as one of the best the agency had. The man had a sensible style. The suit he wore wasn't new, but it was good quality, well-fitted and meticulously maintained. This was someone who took care of his appearance, making sure that he could blend in and wouldn't give himself away. This was someone who took his job seriously.

"I'll have what he's having," Ethan told the bartender when asked.

Darren waited until Ethan's drink arrived before holding his drink up and said, "Cheers."

"Oh, come on," Darren said with a chuckle before pausing to take a sip of the wine. The shiraz was dryer than he normally drank but it was good nonetheless. The food had been excellent; he could see why they dared to charge an arm and a leg for it. "You have to admit that it was pretty stupid sinking all that cash to try and save something that was essentially an unsalvageable black hole."

"Yes, but they couldn't just ignore them, could they?" Ethan tried to argue.

"Of course they could," Darren rolled his eyes. "If they had the guts they would've."

"Okay, fine, you win." Ethan chuckled. He took a peek at his watch before he continued, "It's only nine thirty, still early. You want to go for a walk?"

Darren had thoroughly enjoyed Ethan's company, and he wanted to spend more time with him before they made their way back. He shrugged, giving Ethan a faint smile. "Sure. I could use some fresh air."

Heading out of the restaurant, they walked along the street until they hit Broadway.

"I'd forgotten how vibrant and full of life this place is," Ethan said with a sigh as they strolled through Times Square in the Friday evening crowd. "Even in the winter."

"It's a tourist trap," Darren pointed out.

"Yeah, but that doesn't mean it isn't cool." Ethan looked up at the colorful displays. "I haven't been down here in years."

"You don't come here for New Year's Eve?" Darren asked curiously. Ethan looked like the kind of person that would.

"I'm usually working on New Year's Eve," Ethan shook his head, smiling. "Plus, like you said, it's a tourist trap. I have no interest in lining up for hours just so I can stand on my feet for a few more."

"True," Darren chuckled. "Once is more than enough."

"Speaking of tourist traps—" Ethan waved down a cab.

"Where are we going?" Darren asked as Ethan pulled him into the cab.

"Somewhere I haven't been since I was a kid," Ethan said with a wicked grin before turning to the cabbie. "Rockefeller Center."

Darren felt mesmerized by the man's excited smile. "You do realize I have a driver waiting for us, right?"

"Yeah, but it's faster this way." Ethan shrugged.

The cab dropped them off a few minutes later at their destination. Darren watched Ethan's blue eyes take on a cheerful glow as they stood in front of the giant Christmas tree. He silently reached for Ethan's hand and smiled as he felt Ethan squeeze back.

"You skate?" Darren asked. Maybe it was seeing all those people on the ice, or maybe he was influenced by Ethan's youthful enthusiasm, but he suddenly itched to get out there on the ice.

"I did," Ethan said, sounding a little distant before he looked up at Darren. "It was a long time ago."

"You want to try?" Darren tipped his head towards the rental booth.

"I don't know. I told you it was a long time ago."

"Come on, I'll lead you," Darren said, giving their joint hand a shake. "And I'll catch you, won't let you fall on your butt."

"Oh, all right." Ethan chuckled.

They paid for entry and for the rental, and before long, they were standing on the ice.

"Okay, keep your knees bent and your feet apart." Darren held both of Ethan's hands and gave him instructions. "Yes, that's it. Now push backwards and outwards with your right leg then your left."

He skated backwards, pulling on Ethan's hands as Ethan skated wobbly forward. "There you go! See? You're doing it."

Darren watched Ethan's wide smile contently as they glided across the ice, dodging other skaters as they moved. He breathed deep as brisk evening air graced their faces.

They stopped at the side of the rink for a break to catch their breaths.

"Wow!" Ethan wobbled for a second. Darren grabbed onto his arms to straighten him up.

"You okay?"

"Yeah, I'm good—"

Ethan tripped again, loosing his balance completely this time. Darren tried pulling him in, but lost his own footing too instead. The two of them landed in a heap with Darren on his back and Ethan on top of him. They stared at each other in shock, and there was a silence before they both began to laugh uncontrollably.

"Ow," Darren groaned as they rolled onto their sides.

"Oh my god, I'm so sorry," Ethan said between bouts of laughter as he tried to get up. "Are you okay?"

"Yeah, I'm fine, I think." Darren got back on his feet then pulled Ethan upright. "You?"

"I'm okay." Ethan patted the bits of snow from his coat before doing the same for Darren. "I think we should call it a night, at least for skating," he said, still chuckling. "Before someone breaks something."

"You sure?" Darren wrapped his arms around Ethan's waist, pulling him in.

Ethan nodded before looking up, locking gaze with Darren. The bright lights on the giant tree reflected in Ethan's eyes. Darren was transfixed by the lights dancing in those blue orbs.

Their lips touched. The softness Darren felt on his lips prompted him to go deeper, licking his tongue into Ethan's warm mouth. Their tongues fluttered and danced as they both forgot to breathe.

Darren touched his forehead to Ethan's as their lips finally parted. He felt light-headed, and not just from the lack of air. He was drunk on the man in his arms, intoxicated by his exuberance and bedazzled by his mystique.

"Come on," Darren said after a long moment, his voice low and raspy. "Let's go home."

Darren looked at Ethan as his driver Bobby took them towards his home in the Upper East Side. Ethan's attention was directed at something out the window, although it didn't appear to be anything in particular.

He hadn't expected the night to happen as it did—well, he had no idea how the night could've gone, but skating at the Rockefeller Rink wasn't what he'd expected. The spontaneity had been a welcomed surprise.

Darren smiled faintly as he relaxed in his seat, his eyes still focused on Ethan. Ethan, without a doubt, was a good-looking man, but there was something about the man that made him want to dig deeper, to find out more. It was like there was a whole other hidden side to the man; something more than the playful yet mature image he portrayed for his boyfriend persona.

Ethan was an enigma that pulled at Darren's curiosity.

The kiss wormed its way back into Darren's thoughts. It'd surprised him that a simple kiss like that had had such an enormous effect on him. Darren had felt himself beyond aroused by the kiss they'd shared, and it made him want more. A lot more.

Bobby dropped them off at the door of his building, and the doorman came to greet him, opening the door for them. He looked with interest at Darren's arm around Ethan's waist but said nothing aside from a simple greeting, as he should.

Once they were in his apartment, Darren helped Ethan out of his coat, hanging it in the closet before doing the same with his own. He led Ethan into the living room.

"Make yourself comfortable," he said before he padded towards the open kitchen, taking off his suit jacket and rolling up his sleeves at the same time. "You want anything to drink?"

"What are you drinking?" Ethan asked as he browsed Darren's enormous bookshelf.

"Scotch."

"I'll have one too, then. Straight up."

Darren poured a finger of the amber liquid into each glass before making his way towards Ethan, glasses in hand.

"See anything you like?" Darren muttered against Ethan's ear as he handed a glass to him, then wrapped his free hand around Ethan's waist. He took a sip from his own glass.

The lingering scent of the man's cologne tickled his nose, sending a warm pulse down to his belly, arousing him. He closed his eyes briefly as he took a deeper breath.

"Just admiring the volumes," Ethan said as he turned to face Darren. He sipped from the glass as he stepped closer to Darren.

"I want to thank you," Darren said, letting his fingers dance over Ethan's dress shirt, massaging the younger man's waist lightly, "for a wonderful evening."

"The night is still young," Ethan replied, taking Darren's hands into his own, letting their fingers entwine. He reached up and placed a feather-light kiss on Darren's lips.

Nate stared out at the lights of the city as they drove through Midtown. His thoughts kept wandering back to Darren and the kiss they'd shared earlier. He could still feel the solid warmth under his hand when he tripped on the ice and fell on top of Darren. The same solid warmth as when Darren had wrapped him in his arms, kissing him.

The picture from the file Darcy had sent him, didn't do Darren justice. The man was so much more than a pretty face in a nice suit. Perhaps it was because of the circumstances under which they'd met, but the man had a hidden playful side that was a stark contrast to the hint of darkness on the surface. Nate doubted that most people, even those closest to him, were aware of the Darren's hidden qualities.

It wasn't his place to question his clients' intentions, but Nate couldn't help wondering why Darren had hired him. Darren could've had anyone he wanted.

The man, quoting a friend of his, was gorgeous. Six feet and change in height; the man was muscular and solid, and he had a face that belonged on the cover of a fashion magazine. His dark brown eyes were magnetic; it was difficult to look away from them. Broodingly handsome was barely enough to describe the man.

The driver, whose name was Bobby, as Nate found out, dropped them off at the door of Darren's building. Darren waited for him to get out of the car before extending his arm over Nate's waist. Nate was surprised to find that neither Bobby nor the doorman had commented on that.

The first thing Nate noticed about Darren's apartment wasn't how spacious it was. Most men he'd engaged were of a certain class, so he'd seen his share of penthouse apartments. The first thing Nate noticed was the giant wall of books in the living room. He couldn't help being drawn to those shelves.

The man had a collection ranging from social theory to music and arts to—he chuckled—Harry Potter.

He felt Darren come to a stop next to him, handing him a glass with a splash of Scotch. Darren's hands were back on his waist, his fingers playing lightly with the fabric of his shirt. "See anything you like?"

Nate turned, taking a sip from his glass as he looked up at Darren. *Definitely*, he said to himself; yet another man who he wouldn't mind having a real relationship with in another life. Instead, he shook his head softly. "Just admiring the volumes," he answered as he stepped closer to Darren.

"I want to thank you for a wonderful evening," Darren said, his voice taking on a dark, raspy quality.

Nate wanted to say that it was his job, but it didn't seem appropriate. The truth was he'd had a good time himself too—that, and he didn't want this to be just a "job", for reasons he'd rather not think about.

"The night is still young," Nate said instead.

He took Darren's hand from his waist into his own hand, threading their fingers, before reaching up and pressing his lips to Darren's in a light, gentle caress. Darren leaned in for more, but Nate pulled away. With Darren's hand still in his, he led Darren slowly back towards the black leather couch before pushing Darren to sit down.

Darren took a big gulp of his drink then set it aside. He brought the back of Nate's hand to his lips for a gentlemanly kiss before pulling Nate forward to straddle his lap. Nate put his drink on the side table next to Darren's. Nate let Darren slide his jacket off, tossing it aside, before resting his arms over Darren's shoulders, leaning in for a kiss.

The kiss began slow, just brief touches of their lips, until Darren's hands found their way to Nate's sides and slid up his back. Darren fixed a hand over Nate's nape, pulling him closer to explore the depths of his mouth. Nate could taste the Scotch on Darren's tongue—salty, smoky, with a bit of fruit. Their tongues danced as Darren's large hands roamed Nate's backside. And Nate felt his body heating up as he slowly became aroused.

His hips undulated to a slow, unknown rhythm as he threaded his fingers into Darren's perfectly styled hair. The soft strands sliding through his fingers felt like silk. He moaned softly as Darren's hands moved down to his buttocks, cupping one in each hand and squeezing firmly.

Nate trailed his kisses down the corner of Darren's lips. The stubble on the side of the man's face pricked as he licked and nipped his way down to his neck. Darren tipped his head back, giving him room to roam. Nate trailed his tongue over a spot on Darren's neck, and felt the man's body jolt lightly with a soft gasp. He grinned and continued to nibble and suck at that spot.

He pulled open Darren's silver Zegna tie before working on the dark material of the shirt. Dropping to the floor on his knees, he dragged his tongue over the hard lines of Darren's lightly haired chest after quickly undoing the buttons. He could tell that Darren worked out regularly from the tight, muscular chest and firm eight pack. He caressed the hard washboard abs as his lips reached for Darren's nips.

"Yeah… that's it…" Nate heard Darren groan as his lips came to the man's right nipple, flicking the bud with the tip of his tongue until it was erect. He reached for Darren's left nipple, pinching and playing with the half-hard man nip, drawing out another gasp.

Darren reached for Nate's hair, threading through the tussled locks for a tight grip as Nate kissed his way down Darren's happy trail.

Nate could feel Darren unconsciously rocking his hips, looking for more. He undid Darren's pants and slid the soft material down. The man's cock was thick and long, stretching against the black cotton of his boxer briefs. Nate's mouth watered at the sight of the man's thickness. He licked the sides of Darren's cock, wetting the cotton with his saliva before fixing his lips tight around the head, sucking lightly to stimulate the hard flesh. He nuzzled at the thick length, letting the pungent scent of the man's playground and the sweet smell of pre-cum permeate his senses.

He pulled Darren's shorts down and got rid of them along

with the pants. Darren spread his legs wide to let Nate get at his goodies. Nate licked a streak up Darren's inner thigh, then teased his round balls with his tongue as he buried his nose into the trimmed playground. Darren grunted as Nate sucked gently at his boys.

He felt Darren's hand tighten over his hair, "Open."

Nate looked up and found Darren holding the base of his cock with his free hand. Darren's cock was long and smooth with a flared, plump head. Nate opened his mouth obediently and let Darren feed him his thick shaft.

He bobbed his head up and down as far as he could without gagging. Darren's hand remained tightly over his hair, directing his head gently as he serviced the man.

"Oh… yeah…" Nate heard Darren grunt out as the man began thrusting lightly up into his mouth. "Take that, boy."

There was something about being nearly fully dressed and sucking on someone's cock that always made Nate hot and bothered. His cock throbbed in his dress pants, aching for attention. He gripped Darren's hip with one hand and reached down to undo his pants with the other as he continued to suck at Darren's cock.

He moaned around Darren's thickness as his fingers wrapped themselves over his own shaft. His eyes fluttered shut as he began to stroke himself.

Nate moaned in protest when Darren pulled him off of his cock.

"Strip," Darren ordered. "Slowly. I want to see you…"

Nate grinned. He stood up from where he was kneeling and began working the buttons of his shirt open one by one while swaying his body gently. He reached in to play with his own nipples, gasping and sighing with pleasure as his fingers twisted and pulled at the buds.

He shrugged off the shirt, leaving his tie around his neck, and tossed the shirt to one side.

Darren reached for his cock and jacked himself as he watched Nate dance for him, slowly removing the last bits of his clothing. When Nate was done, Darren reached for the tie still around his neck.

Nate climbed back on the couch, straddling Darren's legs when Darren pulled him close by his tie. He moaned softly at the sensation of their dicks sliding against each other.

"God, you're beautiful," Darren said as he loosened the tie, slipping it off Nate's neck and tossing it behind him.

Nate leaned in for a kiss, letting his tongue play with the other man's. Darren caressed Nate's back gently before moving down to cup the round bubbles of his ass. Nate panted against the side of Darren's face when a digit probed his entrance teasingly. He held onto Darren's neck and began rubbing up against him, looking for more friction, more contact, more… anything. He let out a series of gasps and moans against Darren's cheek when the man's finger probed deeper into him.

He hadn't felt so desperate with a client in a long time. Nate buried his face into the side of Darren's neck and almost begged.

"Come on," Darren said in a raspy voice. "Let's move somewhere a bit more comfortable. Hmm?"

Nate let Darren lead him into the bedroom and push him down on the soft bed. He watched Darren as he shrugged off the black shirt that was hanging from his shoulders and made his way to the bed.

Darren leaned down to kiss Nate, deep and urgent this time.

The heated desires in those dark eyes were unmistakable and overwhelming as Darren wreaked havoc on Nate's senses.

Nate groaned when he felt the plump head of Darren's thick, slick cock invade his ass. He was naturally tight so it burned slightly as Darren entered him, but the discomfort quickly turned into pleasure as Darren began to thrust shallowly, coaxing him to open up. He reached up for Darren as the man began to speed up, pulling him down for more kisses as Darren pushed his long legs against his chest. He groaned in ecstasy with Darren's every thrusts, deeper and more powerful each time.

"Oh god…" Nate cried out, reaching up to grab onto Darren's arms, fingers digging into the solid flesh of his biceps. He could feel his climax starting to build with each stab of Darren's thickness.

"Fuck!" Darren groaned, pulling out and flipping Nate onto his hands and knees before plunging back into Nate. His powerful thrusts sent Nate stumbling forward onto his shoulders. Nate buried his head into the bed, moaning continuously as his fingers scrabbled over the sheets for something to grab onto.

Nate reached one hand under his body and began stroking himself. He was close, lingering right there on the edge. His hands quickened to follow Darren's rhythm, stroking up and down his throbbing hardness. He could feel his balls begin to tighten as his orgasm took over his senses. "Oh fuck!" he cried out as his eyes rolled back, and shot his warm cream all over the sheets beneath him.

Darren's grunts grew louder as his thrusts became more and more erratic. "Oh god, I'm coming!"

The man behind him gave one last powerful thrusts and froze inside of him as he pumped his hot cum deep into Nate's bowels. "Fuck!"

Darren collapsed on top of Nate, both of them breathing heavily as they tried to recover from their intense orgasms. He reached for Nate's hand, holding it tightly with their fingers entwined. Rolling onto his side, Darren pulled Nate's back against him and wrapped him in a tight, possessive embrace as they basked in the afterglow of sex.

It was a while before either man could muster enough brain cells to form any sort of coherent sentence.

"That was…" Nate began, but lost his train of thought when Darren's fingers began absentmindedly tracing circles on his sweaty chest.

"Amazing? Fantastic?" Darren suggested as he nipped at the back of Nate's neck. "Mind-blowing?"

"Any and all of the above." Nate smiled brightly as he turned, reaching his head back to give Darren a soft kiss.

Darren simply deepened the kiss. He asked, after their lips finally parted, "So did I pass the grade?"

"Top of the class, babe," Nate chuckled as he answered.

"Good." Darren sighed against Nate's neck. "Who are you, really? Ethan can't be your real name."

"No, it's not." Nate replied, staring up at the ceiling as he lay in Darren's arms.

"So? Who lives in here behind the mask called Ethan?" Darren asked, gentle but insistent, as he tapped Nate's chest where his heart was with two fingers. "Come on. Please? Tell me your real name."

Nate sighed. He could tell that Darren was genuinely curious by his tone of voice; there was no malice in his intentions. However, it was a very personal question to ask and Darren really had no right to ask him about it.

Somehow though, Nate didn't feel like refusing the man's request. *I must be crazy*, Nate thought to himself. "You do know the point of using a fake name is to maintain the illusion of this whole arrangement, right?"

"Don't you ever get tired of it, though? Pretending to be someone you're not, I mean. Pretending to be someone else's ideal." Darren propped his head up on his hand, looking down into Nate's eyes as he brushed a couple strands of stray hair away.

"I'm not allowed to get tired of pretending," Nate said. It was the reality of his business—he lived and worked for the illusion.

"You don't have to pretend, you know," Darren said. "Not with me."

Nate didn't answer. Sometimes he wondered if he'd been pretending for too long, to the point where Nathaniel had started to resemble the different versions of Ethan more and more. He could no longer see himself clearly when he looked into a mirror; he couldn't tell whether it was Nathaniel or Ethan looking back at him.

He shivered at the thought of it.

"I didn't hire you for the *ideal*." Darren tightened his arm around Nate. "Back there, at the Rockefeller Plaza—that wasn't Ethan who dragged me down three blocks in a cab just to look at a Christmas tree. That was *you*, wasn't it? Whoever *you* are."

Nate's breath quickened. How…

"I have tried everything, and it has always ended the same way. I'm done looking for my happily ever after." Darren let out a long sigh. "All I want right now is something real, with no pretenses, no masks."

Nate looked over at Darren, and was surprised at the hidden despair he saw in the depth of the man's dark eyes.

"Can you do that for me?" Darren asked, his voice subdued and quiet. "Can you be real? For me?"

Nate's heart pounded in his chest. He had heard his share of true confessions from Darren's kind of people, but none of them had had as strong an effect on him as what Darren had just said.

Darren was baring it all for him to see.

Could he? Could he shed all of his masks and diligence and just be himself?

Would he be able to do it without losing what was left of himself in the process?

"It's Nathaniel, Nathaniel de Luca." Nate found himself saying before he could stop the words from tumbling out of his mouth. *Shit.*

"Nathaniel." A small smile lit up Darren's face. "I like it."

Nate shrugged. "Everyone calls me Nate though."

"You don't like Nathaniel?"

"Oh, I do. Sounds kind of like a vampire or a werewolf, doesn't it?" Nate smiled. "But it's long and everyone spells it wrong. Nate's simpler."

"I suppose." Darren nodded. "So where's Nathaniel de Luca from, originally?"

"Jersey," Nate answered truthfully. Now that Darren knew his real name there was no point hiding anything. "You know, you could've just hired an investigator if you wanted my background. Even if I was using a fake name it wouldn't be too hard for them to track that information down."

"True, but I want to hear your version." Darren shifted closer to Nate, draping an arm back over Nate's waist as he pressed light kisses to Nate's shoulder. "I love a good story."

"What am I, your personal modern day Scheherazade?" Nate scowled.

"You're gonna tell me stories for one thousand and one nights?" Darren quipped.

"Maybe, but not tonight," Nate said with a yawn. He rolled on to his side before sitting up. "This Scheherazade is too tired to tell stories at the moment. You're gonna have to wait until tomorrow. I'm gonna take a hot shower and pass out for a few hours."

Darren buried his face into the warm spot Nate had left behind to muffle his chuckles.

"And you can either join me," Nate tossed out with a wink as he sauntered in all his naked glory towards what looked to be the bathroom, "or you can stay where you are and miss out."

3

"WHERE DID THAT..." Nate muttered to himself as he shifted through the big closet that took up a good chunk of floor space in his bedroom. Suits and other sophisticated clothing of various colors hung from the rack. "I remember leaving it here after I got it back from the cleaner..."

His phone buzzed in his pocket. "Hello?" he answered without looking at the screen, and let out a frustrated sigh.

"Hey," the soft baritone of his lover's voice came through the speaker. "You all right?"

"Hey!" Nate paused what he was doing after hearing Darren's voice. "Yeah, I'm fine. Just having trouble finding something in my closet."

"What was it?"

"Nothing," Nate sighed. "Just my big blue scarf."

"You mean the thing that looked like you stole it from the Cookie Monster?" Darren laughed. "You left it at my place. It's in the front hall closet, in the big basket up top."

"What do you have against my scarf?" Nate pouted. "It's big, it's warm, and I like it."

"Okay…" Nate could practically *hear* Darren's eyes rolling over the phone. Darren hated that scarf but Nate couldn't bear to part with it, especially on the colder days. "What're you doing tonight?"

"The usual," Nate answered, holding the phone between his ear and shoulder as he picked up random articles of clothing and books off the floor, putting them back where they belonged. "Was thinking about picking up a few things from the market before I head over to your place."

"Ooh, dinner! Lucky me," Darren chuckled. "But unfortunately, we'll have to postpone that until tomorrow?"

"Why?"

"One of my best friends is a photographer and his new exhibit is opening down in SoHo tonight," Darren said, then paused. He said something indistinct away from the phone before he came back on. "I was thinking… we could grab dinner down that way, then head over to say 'hi'."

Darren added before Nate could respond, "I remember you saying you liked photography. I thought I'd be nice to do something different."

Nate was speechless. He'd only casually mentioned that he enjoyed looking at photographic art when they were chatting one night. He hadn't thought Darren would remember such a small detail like that.

"So? What do you think?" Darren asked, after a lack of response from Nate. "If you want to just stay in, we could do that too."

"Yeah, sure!" Nate smiled at Darren's thoughtfulness. "So where should I meet you?"

"Let's meet back at my place, say five thirty?" Darren said

after a moment.

"Ooh, someone's getting out of work early for once?"

"Nah." Darren sighed. "I'm just clocking out early. I'll be paying for it tonight when we get home."

"Ouch." Nate winced. "Why not just leave from work directly?"

"I need to change into something more comfortable. This suit is killing me."

Nate chuckled. He'd never seen a business man who hated wearing a sharp suit this much. "But you look nice in it. I love a man in a nice suit."

"Still uncomfortable though."

"All right, lover boy. I'll see you at home," Nate said with a small smile, hanging up.

He sat at the edge of the bed, then let himself fall onto the mattress. The springs creaked as the bed took his weight.

It'd been two weeks since their first "date", and things had been going pretty well.

Darren was a busy man, running a company that large. He worked long hours, so really, they didn't spend a whole lot of time during the week. Darren had given him the freedom to do whatever he wanted when he was at work.

"You don't have to be at my beck and call, you know. Just do whatever you want. Whatever you usually do." Darren had laughed when Nate had asked Darren what he wanted him to do when he was at work.

On the weekend though, they'd spent practically every moment together, either lounging at Darren's place or out and about doing something fun.

Like a real couple.

Nate shook his head and reminded himself again that none of this was real. It was never supposed to be. Money changed hands, and he was providing a service. That was all. He might've made it look real, but anything between them would've still been built on a foundation of money.

His mind wandered back to what Darren had said, and he still couldn't believe Darren remembered things he'd only casually mentioned. The man was attentive and that alone made him a good lover. Nate was shocked when Darren confessed to him that his past lovers were all more interested in his money than him.

Why would anyone give up someone like Darren? Nate shook his head, baffled.

Sitting up from the bed, he began stuffing things—clothes, mostly, into his duffel. Despite Darren's busy schedule, Nate had been spending more and more nights at Darren's place. They didn't always have sex; sometimes they just cuddled in bed and talked. He wondered if that was a good thing or a bad thing.

He stared at the swirling abstract patterns on his phone's home screen. It was a week to Christmas, and it felt weird that he wasn't scrambling to get all of his appointments booked and organized through to the new year. Normally, he'd be trying to schedule in as many clients and gigs as possible this time of the year. The holidays were usually a busy season for someone in his line of work, and the money was always good.

Darren hadn't said anything about his plans for Christmas, though. Probably going away to spend it with family, Nate thought.

What would he do with a week off if Darren had decided to visit family?

He always visited his aunt at the home for Christmas Eve and sometimes Christmas Day, but aside from that, there really wasn't much he could do. He'd lost his parents at a young age, and his aunt was the one that raised him. He always made a point of visiting her as much as he could manage, even if she didn't recognize him anymore because of her illness.

Shaking his head, Nate decided to deal with it when the time came. He had to get going if he was going to be at Darren's place on time. New York traffic was a bitch during rush hour.

Darren smiled as he put down his phone, staring out the window. The sun was just about to set, and the skyline of New York City was a haze of indigo and orange.

"So? What did your new 'boy toy' say? You guys coming tonight or what?"

"He's not my boy toy." Darren rolled his eyes and turned his chair around to face the woman standing at the door of his office. "And yes, we'll be there."

"Okay, fine, your new beau. That better?" The woman strolled in, closed the door behind her, then plopped herself down on the visitor's chair in front of Darren's desk. She took off her four-inch stilettos and massaged her feet as she continued. "I've been wondering when you'd start bringing him around. I'm dying to meet him."

"Kate..." Darren warned. "Don't even think about it. It's only been two weeks."

"What?" Kate blinked her eyes, fluttering her long lashes innocently. "I didn't say anything!"

Darren arched an eyebrow and glared at her.

"Oh, fine. I promise I'll be good." Kate rolled her eyes. "God, these shoes are killing me."

"Why do you wear them then?" Darren could never understand women's obsession with shoes.

"The same reason you hate those shiny suits but still wear them, my dear brother." Kate put her shoes back on and got up from her seat. "Anyways, I gotta go make sure Kyle's good to go and not tinkering with something else. You know how he is when he gets into it. I'll see you later at the Blue Dot."

"See you tonight." Darren smiled and watched as his little sister strolled out of the room before letting out a long sigh.

The past two weeks with Nate had been... nothing short of amazing. Nate was incredible in bed. He could get hard just thinking about Nate writhing in his bed, lusting and begging for him.

But the man was so much more than just a good lay. Nate was also funny, witty and surprisingly knowledgeable in a wide variety of areas ranging anywhere from philosophy to pop culture. The man was nothing like the lovers he'd had in the past.

Nate obviously needed money, but Darren could tell that it was more than vanity, more than a selfish need for a plush life. He had, more than once, wanted to ask why Nate was in this line of work, but he felt that it was far too personal. He'd already asked enough of Nate by learning his real name; he didn't want to push Nate more than that.

Darren sighed, leaning back in his chair. His thoughts whirled around the image of Nate in his mind—the bright smile when he was happy, the witty glow in his eyes when they debated about things, the little gasps he breathed when he became aroused…

It was far too easy to fall for someone like Nate, Darren realized, and he wished, not for the first time, that the circumstances had been different. He was beginning to wish that this thing between them hadn't been founded on money. It was probably selfish of him, but Darren wanted Nate to stay with him. They'd only been together for two weeks and he was already having thoughts of what it'd be like to have a future with this man. It was crazy, but he wanted Nate to be right there next to him for the rest of their lives.

He sighed as he packed up to leave. His thoughts went back to his plans for tonight. He could only hope that Kate would like Nate. His sister meant well, but she could be a little overprotective sometimes. With his track record of former lovers, she was right to worry about him. He just didn't want his sister's worries to ruin the best thing that had happened in his life in a very long time.

Darren got home a few minutes after five-thirty. He was glad to find Nate already there, curled up on the couch reading as he waited for him. "Hey," Darren dropped a kiss on Nate's head as he walked past the living room. "What are you reading this time?"

Darren could never quite believe Nate's love for reading. It could be Harry Potter or Homer's Odyssey and Nate would devour it.

"*The Shock Doctrine* by Naomi Klein," Nate answered as he tipped his head back and looked up at Darren with a soft smile. "Hey."

Darren couldn't help lowering his head to taste Nate's sweet mouth. "Mmm… I missed you."

Nate closed the book and turned to kneel on the couch. "Me too," Nate said as he leaned over the back of the couch to kiss Darren properly before pulling away. He gave Darren one last sound kiss on the lips before patting his cheek. "Okay. Go change."

"Ooh, bossy." Darren grinned. "I like it."

Rolling his eyes, Nate asked, "What time's the reservation?"

"Six thirty," Darren answered as he headed into the bedroom to change.

"You better hurry up then," Nate called from the living room.

"Yes, my dear," Darren quipped.

They caught a cab to take them to SoHo. Since the restaurant was only a two block walk from the gallery, they decided to walk after finishing their meal.

The temperature outside had been hovering around freezing, and with the snow beginning to fall, the roads had turned into a slushy mess.

"Brrr…" Nate complained as he rubbed his gloved hands together. "God, I hate winter."

"It's not that bad, is it?" Darren arched an eyebrow. "I thought you were born in Jersey?"

"Being born in Jersey doesn't mean I like the cold." Nate gave Darren the side-eye. "Cold is cold."

Darren chuckled, wrapping his arm around Nate, and pulled him closer. "Come on, we're almost there."

The Blue Dot was a private gallery for contemporary art and relatively well known in the artistic circles, although Nate had only ever *heard* of it. He looked appreciatively at the minimalist design of the space.

"Darren!" a cheerful voice sounded from behind them as they checked their coats.

"Tony!" Nate watched as Darren happily greeted his old friend with a bear hug. "God, it's been too long."

"That's because you're a damn workaholic," a woman said as she stopped next to Nate. "Darren, put Tony down. Vince over there is about to go volcanic on your ass."

"No, I'm not! Kate, stop spreading rumors." The four of them were joined by two other men. The one who spoke was a tall, muscular man who reminded Nate of The Rock. "'Sup, D? Good to see you again."

"Same here." Darren laughed. "It's been too long."

"So? Aren't you going to introduce us?" The woman, Kate, folded her arms in front of her and arched one of her perfectly shaped eyebrows at Darren. "I've been waiting for this all day!"

"Kate, you promised to be nice, remember?" Darren returned the eyebrow before pulling Nate close by his shoulders. "Guys, this is Nathaniel."

"Hi," Nate greeted shyly with a smile. "Just call me Nate."

"This guy right here," Darren pointed to Tony, "Is the star of tonight, Tony Petrelli. The big guy behind him is his partner Vince."

"Nice to meet you, Nate," the two men said almost at the same time.

"The loud mouth over here is my baby sister, Caitlin, who also happens to be my VP of human resources."

"Who you calling a loud mouth?" Kate scowled at her brother before reaching out to shake Nate's hand. "Nice to finally meet you, Nate. You can call me Kate. Everyone does."

"And last but not least, Kyle Sommers, my business partner and the co-founder of our little enterprise, the brain behind everything we do. Oh, and my sister's poor husband."

"Hey! I resent that!" Kate jabbed at Darren with her elbow. "Come on, Nate. I'll show you around."

"Kate…" Darren sighed as Kate pulled Nate away by his arm.

"I know!" Kate said as she led Nate through the crowd and away from the others.

Nate browsed through the various pieces slowly. He had a lovely brief chat with Kate before Kate was pulled away by an urgent phone call.

"Hey." Darren appeared next to Nate as Nate stopped in front of a large, framed piece.

"Hey," Nate smiled as Darren wrapped his arm across Nate's lower back.

"What do you think?"

"Tony really is talented." Nate fixed his gaze back on the piece. "I love how he clearly captured the emotions with such simple compositions."

"He really is." Darren nodded in agreement. "You should see the photos he took when he did a stint in Afghanistan as a war correspondent."

"You must be really proud of him."

"I am." Darren smiled softly as they stood and admired the work.

"How did you guys meet?" Nate asked curiously. "I mean, Kate is your sister so that's obvious. What about the rest of them?"

"Well, that's a long story." Darren chuckled as they continued to move through the gallery. "Kyle, Tony and I were in school together at MIT, but we sort of went down different path after we graduated. I went to Harvard for my MBA, Kyle stayed to do his PhD, and Tony decided that he wanted to see the world from a different perspective."

"That's kind of cool," Nate said with longing. "It's nice to have friends who you've known for a lifetime."

"I'm just glad that I still have good friends like them at this point in life." Darren let out a smile, looking towards Tony and Vince before turning his attention back to Nate. "I hope you're having a good time."

"I am," Nate said with a shy smile. "Thank you for bringing me here."

"You're welcome."

"That doesn't look right." Nate's voice pulled Darren away from his thoughts.

"What doesn't look right?" Darren looked back and forth between the papers in his hands and Nate. They had been curled up on the couch since they got back from the gallery. Darren was catching up on work, with Nate snuggled next to him, continuing to read *The Shock Doctrine*.

"That." Nate pointed to a paragraph in the document Darren had in his hands.

"What's wrong with it?" Darren asked after reading it through a couple of times. "Looks fine to me."

"It's fine only if you assume all your costs are the same across different facilities," Nate said as he shifted for a more comfortable position. "But you can't guarantee that. You can get an average based on past performance, but that doesn't take into account any fluctuations due to market conditions."

"Huh, I hadn't thought about that. Thanks," Darren said, a little dumbfounded. The document was only a draft, but the part Nate had pointed out was a simple, and yet erroneous assumption that would've cost them a lot of unnecessary overhead.

Nate chuckled. "That was pretty much the extent of my capabilities. You can only learn so much in two years of undergrad."

"You were a business major?"

"I took some courses. Never finished my degree, though. Had to drop out after two years," Nate said, looking down at his hands. "Family reasons."

Darren wanted to ask, but he stopped himself. It wasn't his place to pry. Though, it pulled at him, the way Nate talked with longing about school and Darren's friendship with Tony and Kyle.

"You ever thought about going back?" Darren put down the file he was reading and wrapped his arm around Nate.

"All the time," Nate said, snuggling closer. "I will, eventually. Just not right now."

"Is that why you love reading so much?"

"You noticed, huh." Nate chuckled. "That's part of it."

"What's the other part?"

"It helps my business by being able to carry on an intelligent conversation with people."

"Oh." He hadn't thought about that.

"Yeah." Nate shrugged and buried his nose back into the book he was reading.

It was much later when Darren felt a weight on his shoulder. He looked to his shoulder to find the younger man leaning against him, fast asleep. The book Nate had been reading had fallen onto the seat next to them. Darren tossed the work files onto the coffee table. It was late. He could finish the rest tomorrow.

The lines around Darren's eyes softened as he looked closely at Nate's face. He loved watching Nate sleep. Nate always looked so content and peaceful when he slept, like he didn't have a care in the world.

Nate shifted in his sleep, nuzzling against Darren's shoulder.

"Nate? Baby?" Darren touched the side of Nate's face, his thumb brushing Nate's cheeks. "Come on. Wake up."

"Hmm?" Nate answered with a soft moan.

"Come on, let's get you into bed." Darren helped a half-asleep Nate up, then walked him into the bedroom. Nate was back in slumber the minute his head touched the pillow. Darren shook his head with a smile.

Stripping them both down to their shorts, he slid into bed and wrapped his arm around Nate, pulling Nate towards him. Nate turned, pressing his face to Darren's chest then wrapped an arm around Darren, so tight like he was never letting go.

Darren sighed contently at the warm heat of Nate's body.

"If I asked," Darren whispered softly against Nate's forehead as he brushed a fallen strand of hair from Nate's sleeping face. "Would you stay?"

Nate leaned his head on the glass window of the bus as it drove along the quiet residential road.

He'd woken up this morning in Darren's bed, but he didn't remember going to bed. Darren was already gone by the time he got up. The man had left a note by his phone on the bedside table.

"Hey sleepyhead," the note had said in Darren's chicken scratch, "I have to head into the office for a few hours, but hopefully I'll be home by noon. I'll see you then. Kisses."

Nate remembered shaking his head when he saw the note. Who left people notes anymore? Most people just texted these days. He chuckled at the hopelessly romantic side of the man. It was adorable and surprising, to say the least.

By the time he was done his morning routine, it was already ten. With two hours to kill and not much to do, Nate decided to visit his Aunt Rosie. He hadn't been to see her since before Darren happened to him.

The bus dropped him off in front of the hospice facility.

"Nate! Hey!" the plump black woman at the nurse's station greeted Nate as he came into the ward. "How ya doin', love? Haven't seen you here for a couple weeks."

"Hey Sharon. Yeah, I've been pretty busy lately with work." Nate smiled softly as he gave the woman a kiss on the cheek and a big hug. "How's the family?"

"Doing well. You know how it is." Sharon gave Nate a pat on the shoulder as she carried on. "The little ones couldn't wait til Christmas."

"You taking any time off this year?" Nate asked. Sharon was

from New Orleans, and even though she had her own family here, she missed the family she had down south.

"I can't. We're short-staffed for the holidays, so I volunteered to work extra hours." Sharon shrugged. "My oldest will be in college next year. I could use the extra money to get him something nice. Maybe a new computer for school."

"Oh my goodness, has it been that long?" Nate exclaimed. Sharon had worked at the home for many years, and Nate had known her since his aunt moved there.

Sharon laughed. "Oh yes, my boy."

"My… time flies, doesn't it? Anyways, I won't keep you. I'll head down there and find Aunt Rosie." Nate smiled. Sharon had helped him a lot in the past several years after his aunt's condition worsened to the point where he could no longer care for her on his own while holding a job, and needed to be in a care facility.

"Hold up, Nate." Nate paused and turned when Sharon called for him. "Something you need to know, hon."

"What is it?"

"I just got the latest evaluations back. Rosie's condition has gotten worse since she was tested last. I know we've been talking about this every year, but I just want you to be prepared for the eventuality." Sharon held Nate's hand, patting it softly. "The doctors are giving her maybe another year or two."

Nate sighed. "It's okay. I know. It's unavoidable." He shook his head. He knew that day would come, eventually. Rosie was diagnosed with Alzheimer's when he was in his freshman year. It'd been hard to watch her slowly fade away with every visit; Nate had long since accepted that she'd be gone. He just hoped that the end would be peaceful for her.

"I'm so sorry, love. I wish there was more that we could do." Sharon looked at Nate sympathetically.

"It's okay. You've done more than I could hope for already." Nate gave her a small smile. "Thank you, Sharon, for everything. I'll try to come here more often."

"Anytime, love."

"I'll drop by before I leave."

"Sure thing, honey."

Nate strolled down the hall. The hospice was set up more like an apartment building rather than a hospital, which Nate really liked. He knocked on the door of his aunt's room.

"Hey, Aunt Rosie." Nate sat down in the chair facing the woman lying in bed, despite not getting a reaction. He reached out to hold the old woman's hand. "How've you been?"

Rosie looked over at him, but there was no acknowledgement in her eyes. Her lips moved, but all that came out were some faint unintelligible mutterings.

"I met a new friend," Nate said, resting his elbows on the edge of the bed and held Rosie's hand close. "He's really nice, and he loves books, just like you. I think you'd like him."

Nate reached into his messenger bag and pulled out a small book. "I borrowed this from him. Remember this one? You used to read this to me when I was little."

"Oh, totally forgot," he continued. "I have a new project at work. A big project. Remember how you always told me to stick with school? Well, if everything goes well, I'll be able to go back to school after this. I'm excited…"

Nate knew his aunt probably won't understand a word of what he was saying, but he rambled on regardless.

He dropped by to bid farewell to Sharon before he left, and his phone rang just as he was stepping outside.

"Hey," Darren's baritone came smoothly over the phone. "Where are you?"

"Just out for some air, just on my way back," Nate said, stretching his arms and neck to loosen the muscles that had got stiff from sitting too long. "Was thinking about going to the farmer's market. I still owe you a home cooked meal."

"Why don't I meet you down there? We can grab some food before we go shopping."

"Sounds good."

Nate took a deep breath as he hung up. The sky was a brilliant shade of blue as the warm winter sun shone from above, but he couldn't help the feeling of uncertainty in his heart.

4

"HELLO? GUYS?" DARREN yelled as they entered the house. The front of the house was quiet, but Nate could hear the sounds of people talking filtering through the large space of the living room. "Guys? We're here!"

"Darren! Is that you?" a woman's voice rang out. Nate smiled as he recognized Kate's voice. "We're in the kitchen!"

They shrugged off their snow-dusted wool coats and stepped out of their wet shoes before padding through the living room.

Nate hesitated, but Darren's arm around his shoulder prodded him forward.

"Come on, they're all waiting for us." Darren pushed Nate towards the kitchen.

Nate opened his mouth to say something, but then shut it again. It was too late to back out now, so he might as well just go through with it.

He hadn't expected that he'd be spending the holidays with Darren, let alone his two best friend and their better halves. Darren had sprung it on him a few days ago, after asking him what his plans for the holidays were.

"Well, I'd probably go see my aunt at the home on Christmas Eve," Nate had said without looking up. He had been reading in his usual position—snuggled up against Darren—as the man worked on his laptop.

"What about the rest of the week?" Darren asked, playing with Nate's hair absentmindedly.

"I haven't gotten that far yet." Nate closed his book and looked up at Darren. "I thought you were gonna spend the holidays with Kate and Kyle?"

"Well, that was the plan." Darren put his computer on the coffee table before lying back and pulling Nate to lie on top of him. "But Kyle thought that since Tony and Vince are actually in town for the holidays this year, we should all head up to his place in the Hamptons for the week."

"Oh." Nate said quietly, sounding slightly disappointed. So Darren was spending the holidays away after all. Guess he'd have to come up with something to do then.

Darren snuck a finger to Nate's chin and lifted his head. "You're coming too, you know."

"What?" Nate's eyes widened. "Wait, I'm going?"

"Kate's orders," Darren said before leaning his head down to peck a kiss on Nate's lips. "What, you think I'm going to leave you here all by yourself?"

"It's not that..." Nate stumbled over his own words. "I mean, it's your family gathering and all... why me?"

"What do you mean 'why you'?" Darren scowled at him. "Stop being silly. We'll go see your aunt during the day and then drive up to Kyle's place after lunch. It shouldn't take more than a few hours to get there even with traffic."

Darren's arm tightening around his shoulder woke Nate

from his thoughts.

"You okay?" Darren looked at him with concern.

"Yeah, I'm fine." Nate nodded.

"Come on."

Dinner was a team affair. Kate had done all of the shopping days before, but they all chipped in to help with the preparation.

"Oh my god," Kyle said as he lay in a heap on the couch with Tony and Vince. "I can't move."

"You just had to eat the rest of that mashed potatoes, didn't you?" Kate rolled her eyes as she walked past the men with her cup of coffee and settled on the love seat where Nate was. They'd all had quite a bit to drink, so everyone was a little giddy and silly.

"You know I can't say no to it." Kyle gave Kate the puppy dog eyes. "You make the best potatoes, you know that!"

Nate couldn't help laughing. He was stuffed to the gills like the rest of them, but it was worth it. The food had been delicious.

"What's so funny?" Darren asked as he walked into the living room, wiping his wet hands on the back of his jeans. He'd volunteered to load the dishes, and Nate could hear the machine whirring in the background.

"Your brother-in-law," Kate said with a sigh.

"He'll never learn, haven't you realize that already after all these years?" Darren parked himself on the armrest of the love seat next to Nate.

"I give up. Anyone want coffee?" Kate drained her cup in one gulp, getting up.

"You say that every year, Kate." Vince grinned as Tony shifted to lie on top of him. Tony had his camera in his hands and was looking through the pictures they took at dinner time.

"Shut up." Kate glared at Vince.

"I'll come with you. I could use a cup." Nate got up and followed Kate into the kitchen.

Kate set an empty mug on the island counter and filled it with coffee. "How do you take it? Cream is in the fridge, sugar's on the table."

"Thanks, black is fine," Nate said, taking a sip of the black coffee. "And thanks for inviting me, Kate."

"Oh, honey!" Kate smiled as she rested her elbows on the counter. "You're always welcome here. I should be thanking you. I haven't seen my brother this happy in years, and that all happened after he met you."

Nate felt himself flush. He felt guilty about lying to Kate and the others, but what choice did he have? "And you don't mind…"

"What, that you're a guy?" Kate huffed out a laugh. "Honey, I've known Darren was gay since he was sixteen. Not much surprises me these days."

Kate filled her own cup before tipping her head towards the living room. "Come on, you can't leave those boys alone. They'll end up doing something crazy."

Nate chuckled.

Darren was sitting in Nate's seat when he returned to the living room. Darren reached out a hand and pulled Nate into his lap after Nate set his cup down on the coffee table. "Whatever bad things Kate told you about me, they're all lies! Not a word of it is true!" Darren proclaimed.

Nate laughed as he leaned against Darren's solid chest, feeling the warmth radiating through his cloths.

"I did no such thing!" Kate gasped dramatically. "Nate, tell your lover that I didn't say anything bad about him."

"Kate didn't say anything bad about you." Nate grinned up at Darren.

"Oh my god, Kate has corrupted you!" Darren deadpanned, and Kyle, Tony and Vince began laughing uncontrollably. "There is only one way to cure this."

"What... what are you doing?" Nate said, pretending to be scared. He couldn't help playing along; it was too funny not to.

"Why, a kiss of course!" Darren grinned before pulling Nate into a deep, heated kiss.

Darren's kiss was overwhelming, and Nate had almost forgotten about the others as Darren's tongue fluttered in his mouth, teasing and playing with his tongue.

He was out of breath, panting heavily when Darren finally let go of him. The others were blowing wolf whistle around them, and Nate buried his head into Darren's chest as his face flushed bright red.

"All right, guys, we're gonna head to bed." Tony was the first one to bid goodnight after nearly falling asleep in Vince's arms. "See you guys in the afternoon."

"Afternoon?" Kyle snort out a laugh.

"Yup. I'm *not* getting up before noon, if I can help it," Tony said as he headed towards the stairs with Vince. "Night, guys."

"Night."

"I think we're going to hit the sack too," Darren said after watching the guys leave.

"Good idea," Nate answered, letting out a small yawn.

"Good night, Kate, Kyle."

They made their way up the stairs and Darren led him into their room. It was a simple but spacious room with a large window.

The sky was a haze in the shade of dark indigo. The snow had begun to fall again and Nate could barely make out the setting half moon over the tree line as he looked out the window.

Darren came up behind him, his arms circling Nate's waist, as he rested his chin on Nate's shoulder. Nate closed his eyes to feel the man behind him as their bodies swayed together gently in the dark silence.

Nate turned slightly so he could reach up and pull Darren into a searing kiss. Darren's hands began to wander up and down Nate's belly before slipping under Nate's sweater. Nate moaned into Darren's mouth as Darren's fingers began to dance over his torso, rucking up the hem of his sweater.

"I'm so glad you're here," Darren whispered as he spun Nate around, holding Nate tight against him.

Nate could feel Darren's arousal pressing against his own as their hips ground together. "Me too," he answered quietly.

He offered no resistance when Darren began undoing his jeans and taking off his sweater. He shivered slightly as Darren pulled his sweater and t-shirt over his head. His nipples hardened at chill in the air.

Darren slowly undressed him, feeling every inch of his body. Nate moaned and sighed when Darren's fingers lingered over his hot spots. Darren had always been an attentive lover, but this somehow felt different to Nate.

Nate relaxed as Darren laid him down on the bed, and he watched as Darren slowly stripped himself down. He admired

Darren's toned, muscular form as the man slowly made his way to him.

Darren hovered over him, raining gentle kisses on his forehead, temple, eyes, before making his way down to Nate's lips, then jaw. His dark eyes pulled at Nate, like whirlpools of darkness, threatening to take away his soul. He couldn't help the soft whimpers and sighs as Darren kissed his body, his agile tongue lingering over the hot spots on Nate's body.

Darren's hands roamed over Nate's chest, twisting and pinching his taut nipples as he followed the thin trail of ginger hair down to Nate's shaved playground. Nate's throbbing length, slender and smooth, lay full and aching for attention on his belly, but Darren simply kissed and licked around it, moving downwards.

"Mmm…" Nate bit into his lower lip but couldn't stop the loud moaning from escaping his throat. Darren teased the thin skin of his round balls with his tongue, lapping and sucking at them like candy. "Oh…"

Nate hissed when Darren pressed into Nate's tight pucker with his thumb. His muscles tightened around the wide, invading digit.

"Relax for me," Darren growled against Nate's inner thigh as he pushed the leg up and began kissing the soft, creamy skin, dragging his teeth lightly over the surface.

Nate tried to obey and relax his ass but Darren's tongue wandered back to his balls and then lower to suck at his taint. "Oh god…"

Nate could feel Darren's tongue in his ass as the thumb began to push further into him. Darren continued to lick and probe Nate's ass, adding more fingers. The slow, sweet torture was slowly turning Nate into a writhing wreck on the pristine white cotton sheets. "Oh god, Darren!"

When Darren finally pushed into him, Nate felt nothing but pleasure as his lover penetrated him, and a warm fuzzy energy began to collect at the pit of his belly. He wrapped his long legs tightly around Darren's waist as Darren began thrusting into him.

Darren kept his strokes long but powerful, filling Nate with his hardness as he leaned in and took Nate's mouth possessively. His sweaty skin gleamed in the dim light of the room as Nate reached up to hold him, his fingers digging into his shoulder blades.

Bottoming out inside Nate, Darren flipped them both over. The sudden movement caused Darren to sink deeper into Nate, making him cry out with a loud gasp at the sensation.

Nate leaned down, desperately seeking Darren's lips, as he began to roll his hips, riding on Darren's cock. He could feel Darren's hands roaming his back, grasping at his ass cheeks as his hips moved up and down over Darren's shaft. He buried his head into Darren's chest, breathing in the sweaty scent of the man as he moaned and panted heavily, desperate for release.

Darren propped himself up on his arms for leverage, and began to thrust upwards to meet Nate. The sounds of skin slapping skin mingled with the lovers' pants and moans of pleasure.

Nate tossed his head back, supporting himself with a hand on Darren's leg. "Oh my god, I'm so close—"

"Come for me, baby." Darren sat up into a kneel and gripped Nate's hips, pulling him towards him, plunging into him hard and fast. "Oh fuck. I'm coming too…"

Darren pulled Nate hard towards him then froze as he came.

Nate could feel the hot cum coating his anal walls as Darren exploded deep inside of him. "Ahh!"

Darren laid Nate down on the bed and pulled out. His chest heaved as he dragged his tongue over Nate's body down to his cock. Nate groaned as Darren took him into his hot mouth.

"Come on, baby," Darren growled in a low, raspy voice as his hand stroked Nate with a feverish pace. "Let me taste you."

He wrapped his lips around Nate and began to apply suction as he stroked harder and faster. He slid two fingers back into Nate, twisting and pressing over his prostate. Nate's mind blanked as Darren's fingers began rubbing over his secret spot, pushing him over the edge with a choked cry as he filled Darren's mouth with his cream.

After he came to, he was lying on his side with Darren holding him tightly from behind. Darren's hand rubbed soothing circles on his chest.

"You okay?" Darren asked with a slight worry in his voice. He kissed Nate's shoulders as his hands roamed. Nate reached back with his head to meet Darren's lips. He could taste on Darren's tongue the faint brininess of his own cum.

"Yeah. I'm fantastic," Nate answered with a sleepy grin. It hadn't been the roughest sex they'd had, but he was tired. He shivered as his sweaty skin began to cool.

"Come on, let's get under the covers." Darren pulled at the duvet under them.

Nate heard the old grandfather clock on the main floor chime midnight as they got comfortable under the blankets. He looked over to Darren and said sleepily. "It's Christmas Day."

Darren chuckled. "Yeah."

"I never did ask you what you wanted for Christmas," Nate

said.

"I've already got what I wanted right here." Darren leaned in and pressed his lips gently to Nate's. "Merry Christmas, Nate."

"Me too. Merry Christmas to you too." Nate smiled as he drifted off to sleep.

Nate knocked on the frosted glass door before pushing it open slightly to peek in.

Darren looked up from the file he was reading. "Nate! Come on in."

"Here's the file you wanted. I think I've caught everything." Nate dropped the file on Darren's desk before sitting down on the sofa in his office. "There were a few spots that could use some clarification. I added my comments."

"Thanks," Darren said. He pushed away from his desk and moved to sit down next to Nate. "So? What do you think of your first week?"

"Pretty good. I mean, I don't really get to interact with very many people but the ones I've met were pretty nice." Nate smiled as he motioned for Darren to sit up straight so he could fix his tie. "You need to stop fiddling with your tie."

"But it's uncomfortable," Darren complained. "You know, I never had to wear a tie until I was at Harvard."

"Am… I interrupting something?" Kyle's voice almost made Nate jump in his seat.

Nate had been helping Darren with paperwork ever since they got back from the Hamptons. Originally, Nate was a little uncomfortable with the idea since most of the files that came through Darren's desk were the confidential, top secret, eyes-only type. Even though Darren had said he trusted Nate, Nate still wasn't sure it was a good idea.

It all changed when one night, Nate found Darren still slaving away past midnight. Darren's company was poised to go public in the next month or so, which meant that everyone, the president included, had extra homework to do.

After Nate had spent a week helping Darren out at home, proofing and error checking documents and generally putting his prior education to good use, Darren decided that it would be far more effective if Nate were to work for him during the day as his personal assistant.

And the rest, as they said, was history.

"Depends on your definition of something," Darren quipped, folding his arms in front of him. "What is it?"

"Nothin'," Kyle shrugged. "I'm on order from my lovely wife to make sure you weren't abusing Nate."

"I would never! Nate, you tell him!" Darren scoffed with an incredulous look on his face, causing Nate to burst out laughing.

"Please tell Kate I'm doing okay, and thanks for checking up on me," Nate said when he finally got his laughter under control. "I appreciate it."

"Just keep doing the good work, kiddo."

"You know, I've never seen Kate take to someone this quickly," Darren said, shaking his head.

"I know, right?" Kyle commiserated. "I feel totally left out, and I'm the husband!"

"What can I say? It's all part of my charm," Nate quipped with a smug grin and a shrug. "Anyways, I gotta get back to work. I'll get the summary on that stack of financial numbers to you later this afternoon."

"Wait, you're forgetting something," Darren said as Nate was about to get up from the couch.

"What did I forget?" Nate frowned.

"This." Darren pulled Nate close by his tie for a kiss before letting him go.

"Geez, guys, can you at least wait until I'm gone?" Kyle rolled his eyes. "This is still business hours the last time I checked."

"You only say that because you're jealous." Darren grinned unrepentantly. "Right, Nate?"

"I'm not getting into this." Nate chuckled as he left the room.

"Hey, Darren?" Nate called out to Darren as he sat cross-legged on the floor with spreadsheets all around him.

"Yeah?" Darren answered, yelling so Nate would be able to hear him over the range hood.

"Who's in charge of the Anderson account?"

"Uhm… I can't remember. I'll have to check with the accounts department. Why?"

"There's a discrepancy here…" Nate hummed. "And here, again. And there."

"Hold on, give me a second." Nate turned to see what Darren was doing but he couldn't from where he was sitting. Turning off the stove, Darren strolled over to the living room. "Where's the discrepancy?"

"Here, I've circled it." Nate handed Darren the piece of paper.

"That looks like business expenses," Darren frowned as he studied the lines of information. "That's the code for travel, food… yeah, looks like expenses."

"Ten grand is a bit high for expenses," Nate said, flipping through the stack of paper in his hands. "They don't match up with the reports from accounting. I see the money disappears here and reappears somewhere else. This has been happening regularly."

"Hmm." Darren pursed his lips as he continued to study the sheet. "Talk to Linda in accounts tomorrow and see who's responsible for that account."

"Yeah, sure." Nate shrugged, rubbing his eyes. He'd been staring at those spreadsheets for too long.

"In the mean time, you are officially done for the day. You've been working too hard."

"I'm not done—"

"I'm the boss, and I say you're done for the day." Darren snatched the papers away from Nate's hand. "Up."

"—yet." Nate sighed when he lost the hold on the spreadsheets. "Fine."

"Come on." Darren pulled Nate to standing and ushered him to the dining table. Nate looked on with interest when Darren lit a pair of candles that were sitting between two place sets.

"Darren?"

"Hmm?" Darren hummed as he set two plates of salad down.

"What's going on?" Nate smirked as Darren pretended to be a sommelier as he poured the wine.

Darren gasped dramatically as he sat down, which made Nate chuckle. "You don't remember?" Darren asked.

"No…? Did I miss something?" Nate frowned. He was usually good with dates.

Darren let out a long sigh. "Two months."

Nate almost yelped when he heard Darren say 'two months'. "Oh my god, I totally forgot about it. I'm so sorry—"

"Hey! Baby." Darren reached across the table to hold Nate's hand, calming Nate down. "It's okay."

Pulling Nate's hand close, Darren pecked a kiss on the back of his hand before letting go. "You were busy. We both were. It's okay, really. We cool?"

Nate nodded.

"Good. Now, eat, before the food gets cold." Darren grinned. "Probably not as good as what you make, but I've been told I make a mean steak."

The ruckus coming from one of the cubicles told Darren exactly where he would find his lover. There was a thick crowd gathered around the cubicle, looking on with an array of expressions. Darren didn't have any problems navigating through the crowd though; as soon as his employees saw him, they simply cleared a path for him to the source of the spectacle.

"What's going on here?" Darren asked. He frowned when he saw Nate's bloody nose and disheveled appearance as he sat on the floor. Darren reached out a hand to pull him to standing. "You all right?"

"Yeah, I'm fine." Nate pulled away and carefully created some distance between them once he found his footing.

A man was kicking and screaming, struggling as two security guards held the man back. "Don't you dare do this to me, you whore!"

Darren could see Nate flinch as the man called out more insults.

"I know all about you, you fag whore!" the man continued, despite the security guard's attempt at convincing him to shut up.

"I have no idea what you're talking about," Nate said, emotionless. Darren could tell that Nate was trying to keep his voice calm, but Darren could hear the uncontrollable shaking as Nate spoke.

"Get him out of here!" Darren ordered, and watched the two guards drag the man to the elevator. He made sure they were gone before he turned to the crowd around him. "What happened here? Someone better have a good explanation for this!"

"Uh…" A guy from the cubicle on the opposite side of the wall spoke up. "Well, Mr. de Luca came to ask Randall a question. I didn't hear what it was, but all of a sudden Randall started yelling, throwing punches. Sally called security as soon as that happened."

"Sally?"

"That's me." A middle-aged woman standing next to Nate gave Darren a small wave as she pulled a tissue from her desk and gave it to Nate. "I was just getting back from the break room when I heard Randall Bartlett start yelling. Nasty language. And then he punched poor Nate here, so I called security."

"Thank you, Sally." Darren gave the woman a polite smile. "You two, I want an incident report on my desk before the end of the day. As for the rest of you, don't you guys have better things to do?"

The crowd dispersed as soon as Darren made it clear that

they should not stick around.

"Nate, you're with me," Darren said as he began making his way back to his office.

As soon as they were back in Darren's office, he shut the door and pulled Nate into his arms. He buried his face into Nate's neck, breathing deeply to take in the man's soothing scent to calm himself.

"Are you all right?" Darren asked softly after letting Nate go. He brought his hand up and gently caressed the side of Nate's face with his fingers. Nate flinched when Darren's hand neared.

Darren was furious. He was angry with that Bartlett guy for hurting Nate, but he was more angry with himself for allowing this to happen.

"Yeah, I'll be fine." Nate said, pulling away from Darren to sit on the couch after grabbing the box of tissue off of the coffee table.

"What happened?"

Nate poked at his reddened cheek, hissing as he answered, "I managed to track down the source of that discrepancy I showed you the other day."

"It was Bartlett?" Darren sat down next to him.

"Yeah. He was taking money out of the account and putting it back in, but I found out a few entries that wasn't returned. If it hadn't been for that, no one would've noticed it." Nate sighed, leaning his head back against the cushion, pinching his nose. "I went to ask him about it… and the rest, you already know."

"You should've came to me first, Nate." Darren sighed.

"I know, I should've. I honestly didn't expect that. I was only going to ask him for his expense records," Nate answered quietly. "I'm sorry, Darren. I messed up."

"That's nonsense." Darren reached over and forced Nate to face him. "You couldn't have known this was going to happen."

Nate didn't answer.

"I'm going to have to bring the cops in on this," Darren said after he thought for a moment. "Come on."

"Where're we going?" Nate asked when Darren pulled him up from the couch.

"Home." Darren watched as Nate's shoulders slump before adding. "This is not a reprimand, silly. We're just going home. And you need to ice that eye, or you'll turn into a big panda by tomorrow."

After they got home, Darren sat Nate down and made sure he iced the bruises. As the adrenaline began to wear off, Nate fell into a light doze on the couch.

Darren sat on the edge of the couch, watching Nate as the younger man dozed. His face still looked bruised but it wasn't as bad as earlier in the day. He reached to gently caress Nate's bruised cheek.

He brushed a few strands of hair away from Nate's face. The younger man kept saying he was going to get it cut and colored, but Darren secretly wished he wouldn't. He liked Nate's natural strawberry blonde hue with a dusting of auburn. And he liked the length, too; it was just long enough to slide softly through his fingers whenever he played with Nate's hair.

Darren withdrew his hand when Nate muttered and turned in his sleep. He didn't want to wake him.

The winter sun had long since set, and the only light in his apartment came from the soft yellow glow of the three pod lights in the living room.

Darren kept thinking back to that afternoon. Even though he knew nothing would've happened, he couldn't help worrying about it. He didn't want to see Nate hurt, ever.

He'd heard what Bartlett called Nate. The fact that he was gay and the fact that he and Nate were bumping boots were open secrets in the office. What the others didn't know was Nate's true profession. He'd seen the way Nate flinched at those insults. Nate had behaved like he hadn't heard the words but Darren knew how much it must've stung.

He wished he could shield Nate from it all. He suddenly felt selfish for asking Nate to give him a hand around the office. He should've known better.

"God, you have it bad for him," Darren muttered to himself. He could no longer deny his feelings for Nate. He had fallen hard, probably since they first met. But did Nate feel the same for him? It was a question Darren didn't have the answer for and didn't dare to ask.

He leaned down to press his lips softly at Nate's temple. "What am I going to do with you?"

Nate sat alone in Darren's apartment. He had his laptop opened to a webcast site where the camera was pointed at a glass podium with logo and the words "Chase Sommers" on the front.

He didn't know why he was nervous. Darren and Kyle would be the one making the speech and taking questions from the reporters, yet Nate felt nervous.

Today was the big day. The day for the big announcement of Darren's company going public with their plans for initial public offerings.

There was some feedback from the microphone and a bit of a scramble as everyone got into position. Nate watched anxiously as Darren strolled onto the stage to stand behind the podium in his usual charming swagger.

"I'm sure all of you have heard about the recent incident involving one of our former employees. Let me assure you that everything has been dealt with and taken care of. At Chase Sommers, we are all about doing what is necessary, especially when it came to our clients," Darren began. "I'm happy to announce today, that after so many years of hard work by our employees, Chase Sommers will finally be taking the next step in expanding our operations. We will be releasing our first block of initial public offerings over the next week."

Darren waited for the crowd to quiet down before continuing. "And now, I'll give the floor to Kyle Sommers, our Vice President of Operations, who will be answering you questions."

A text came into Nate's phone as soon as Darren stepped off the stage.

DONE! Darren texted. *Well, not quite, but I should be able to leave soon.*

Nate chuckled as he texted back. *Time to celebrate?*

Damn right!

When're you gonna be home? Nate asked.

We're actually going out for drinks. Us two, Kyle, Kate, Tony and Vince. At Chianti's in an hour. Darren replied.

Okay, I'll meet you guys there. Nate said before putting his phone down.

They were both laughing and giggling like mad when they came through the door.

"No I did *not*!" Darren scoffed at Nate.

"Oh yes, you did." Nate laughed as Darren wrapped his arm around him and began tickling him.

"I didn't!"

"Tickling is cheating!" Nate cried foul, but Darren was judge, jury and executioner. "Okay! Uncle! I said uncle!"

Darren had a mischievous grin on his face as he pulled Nate upright and leaned him against the wall of the front hall.

"I'm so happy for you," Nate said sincerely when he finally managed to stop laughing. Darren stood close, and their hips bumped when Darren leaned forward to kiss him.

"Thank you," Darren said before tasting Nate's lips again. "For everything."

Nate didn't know how to respond. Instead, he deepened the kiss and let Darren take over when the man began kissing him back deeply and possessively.

Once they began exploring each other's body they couldn't stop. Nate arched his hips forward to grind against Darren's hardening erection as Darren pinned him against the wall.

Their fingers worked clumsily to take each other's clothes off, wanting to get at the skin underneath. They continued to kiss as they made their way into the living room, leaving a trail of clothes behind. They were both completely naked by the time they got to the couch, their hands roaming over each other's chests and backs eagerly.

Nate climbed onto the couch on his hands and knees. Once he was in position he reached for the lube he'd hidden under the couch and began to finger himself as he lay on top of a pile of cushions.

He moaned loudly as he stretched himself. His lips were parted as he looked longingly at Darren, who had begun to stroke his hardness as he watched Nate.

Darren didn't wait for long. Once he saw that Nate was ready with three fingers in his ass, he settled behind Nate, still pumping himself. He pulled Nate's fingers out and plunged into Nate's tight entrance, bottoming out in one long stroke.

They both groaned when Darren slid home. Nate arched back to kiss Darren as Darren began to thrust into him, hard and fast.

"Oh… oh god… Oh yeah…" Nate whimpered against the cushion under him when Darren began jackrabbiting into him. Darren draped his body over Nate, and Nate could feel his lover's body heat branding his back as Darren fucked his ass hard.

Nate gasped and moaned loudly. Darren's passion was overwhelming and Nate felt like he was going to black out from the pleasure Darren was giving him. "Oh yes… God…"

"You like that?" Darren said, his voice dark with lust.

"Oh god, yes!" Nate groaned with Darren's powerful thrusts. "Ahh…"

Nate gripped onto the armrest and began pushing his ass back to meet Darren's thrusts. "Oh my god…"

Darren's hips collided with Nate's ass and the wet sound of skin slapping skin echoed in the room as Nate continued to roll his hips. Nate buried his face into the cushions, letting the soft material muffle his moans and whimpers. "Oh… oh…!"

Darren's hands roamed all over his back before resting on his ass cheeks. They gripped firmly, drawing out more cries of pleasure. Nate could feel the warm glow of his climax building and coiling in his body as his muscles began to tighten.

"Ohhh… god…oh… yes! Oh god, I'm coming…," Nate cried out, looking back at the man that was plunging into him as he came.

Darren followed right behind him, spilling his load all over Nate's back before collapsing on top of him.

Darren reached for his hand, threading their fingers, and held on tight. He kissed Nate's neck and shoulders, like he couldn't get enough of him.

"I love you," Nate heard Darren say, breathlessly. "God, I love you so much."

Nate's heart thumped in his chest when he heard Darren's words. So many emotions warred against each other in his head that he couldn't think straight. He closed his eyes when he felt the moisture begin to collect. He wasn't quite sure if they were the tears of joy or sorrow.

Darren took him again in the shower, pressing him against the steam-warmed tiles of the shower wall, lifting him clean off the ground as he rutted into him. All Nate could do was hold on to the man, like he was a leaf in the wind, as he drowned in the presence of the man and the ecstasy the man brought him.

He blacked out briefly when his orgasm over took him, and by the time he came back to himself, Darren had lowered him back onto the floor. He was held securely in Darren's arms and the man was washing his body lovingly as he pecked kisses onto his shoulders.

That night, Nate lay sleepless in Darren's arms even though he was dead tired from the sex they'd had. Darren's words echoed loudly in his ears, and Nate could feel the tears coming back and threatening to escape.

I love you too, Nate had wanted to say, but he was afraid.

He was afraid of what it would mean.

How did this happen? He was so careful.

You broke your own rule, a voice said in his head. *You need to get out, while you still can.*

But he didn't want to leave. How could he?

You'll have to, another voice sounded in his head.

No!

Nate sobbed silently into the pillow as he felt his heart break into a million shards.

Nate woke up early the next morning and found himself, once again, at Pier 11 overlooking the East River. The water taxis zipped in and out of the slips, leaving nothing but a ripple that would eventually smooth out into nothing.

Kind of like him. Walking through life leaving nothing but a few ripples.

His eyes were swollen from crying himself to sleep, and the chilled air stung his puffy lids.

So this was it, then. Nate took a deep breath to fight back the urge to cry again.

He took his phone out of his coat pocket, and dialed a set of numbers he hadn't had to call in a long time.

"Hello?"

"Darcy," Nate said quietly. "It's me."

"Ethan! Everything all right?" Darcy greeted happily but then he seemed to have sensed the ominous air from across the wires.

"I'm ending this engagement," Nate answered with a sniff of his nose. "I can't… I… I need to get out."

"Ethan?"

"Everything is fine," Nate tried to reassure his agent. "I'm just… tired of this. I'm out."

"What do you mean, you're out?"

"I'm out. As in, I'm quitting." Nate sighed. "Forever. Out of the game. Done."

"Ethan—"

"Don't. Don't try and stop me." Nate stopped Darcy before he could say more. "I told you when I signed on that I can't and won't be doing this forever. It's time."

Darcy sighed. "I know. It's just…"

"Anyways. I called just to let you know I'm out," Nate said. "Try not to miss me too much."

"You know I will, jerk," Darcy quipped, but Nate could hear the regret in his voice.

"I see you around, jackass."

Darren was waiting for him by the time Nate got back to Darren's apartment.

"Where've you been? I woke up and you weren't there—"

"I went for a walk," Nate answered coldly.

"You all right, babe?" Darren pulled Nate into his arms. He was wearing a robe on top of his boxer briefs, and the heat of his chest almost crumbled Nate's resolve. "I'm just worried, that's all."

Nate pushed away from Darren's arms and sat down on the armrest of the couch. He clasped his hands between his knees as he watched Darren pull on a pair of jeans and a sweater. His wavy black hair hung loosely from his forehead and Nate had the sudden urge to brush it back for him.

"I'm leaving," Nate said calmly as Darren came back into the living room.

"What?" Darren froze.

"I said, I'm leaving."

"You're not staying for the rest of the day?"

"No. I'm leaving. Leaving you." Nate closed his eyes as he said. Nate didn't think he could bear looking at Darren as the man realized what he was saying.

"What? Why?"

"This full-time thing just isn't working, Darren." Nate opened his eyes but he couldn't see Darren clearly as moisture began to collect in his eyes.

"Why?" Darren's shoulder slumped like someone had killed his favorite puppy. Maybe what he did wasn't that far off, Nate though to himself. "I thought you were happy here. I thought you were happy with me?"

"It's a good arrangement," Nate heard the speech he'd prepared tumble out of his lips. "But I need to see other clients. This exclusive thing isn't working for me."

Nate stood up, put his hat back on and made his way to the door.

"No, I don't believe that." Darren grabbed onto Nate's wrist, tight enough to be uncomfortable.

"Believe what you want, it won't change a thing," Nate said, trying to pull his wrist back from Darren's hands. "Darcy will be in touch to settle your account."

"Wait!" Darren said. "Just tell me one thing."

"What?"

"Tell me that you don't love me."

I can't, because I do love you, Nate wanted to say, but he knew he couldn't.

Instead, he said, calmly, "I've never loved you."

He struggled out of Darren's hold on his wrist and ran out the door. Riding in the elevator down to the lobby, he could no longer stop the tears from spilling out. He sobbed and banged his fist on the brass panels of the elevator as he slid down to the floor.

The elevator dinged as it arrived at the lobby. Wiping his tears, he walked quickly out of the elevator towards the door.

"Nate! Wait!"

Darren's voice sounded from behind him as he stood by the road to hail for a cab.

"Darren, I told you—"

"I don't care. I don't believe that you never loved me." Darren leaned forward and kissed him. "I know, in my heart, that you love me. I just know."

"Let go." Nate struggled against Darren's hold. "Let go of me!"

"No. I will never let go."

Nate yanked his arm harder and finally pulled away from Darren.

And into oncoming traffic.

5

THE LAST THING Nate remembered before the darkness was the bright light in his eyes. He woke slowly, confused. He blinked open his eyes but he could barely keep them open.

There were noises around him. Lights. And people talking. Shouting.

And everything hurts.

He groaned then shut his eyes again. If he wasn't awake it wouldn't hurt as much, right?

He woke again and he was somewhere else. There were still people around him, but everything was swaying from side to side. He didn't hurt as much as before—in fact, he felt euphoric and kind of giddy—but he was just so damn sleepy.

And then, he was lying back, with rows of harsh overhead lights running past him.

"What do we have?"

"Vehicular accident. Patient is a Caucasian male, five-eleven, a hundred and seventy pounds. BP is low at ninety over sixty, but holding steady. Possible mild concussion. Nothing seems broken but he was in and out of consciousness the whole time."

"All right, let's get him on the bed."

He groaned at the pain as they moved his body, then passed out again.

When he came to, he could hear things beeping around him, like an artificial symphony. He groaned at the stiffness in his body as he tried to raise his head.

He still ached all over, but it was dull and muted somehow. Except for his head—it felt like his skull was about to split open.

"Oh, good, you're awake," a cheerful female voice said, which made him look to the left. The woman had a pair of scrubs on. Must be one of the nurses, he thought.

"What happened?" He tried to raise his hands before he noticed the IV that was going into the back of his hand.

"You were in an accident. Got hit by a car." The nurse answered. "You were lucky though. Nothing broken except for a sprained ankle and some scrapes and bruises. You do have mild concussion though. That's what's causing the headache."

"Where's my phone?"

"Here. All of your stuff is in this bag." The nurse dug a clear plastic bag filled with his things out from the closet. "You're going to have to stay for another twenty-four hours for observations because of the concussion, so I suggest you get comfortable."

Nate sighed as he slumped back into bed. Great.

"I'll come by again when the IV's done," the nurse said as she checked off a few things on his chart. "By the way, I'm Daphne, just in case you need to get a hold of me."

"Nice to meet you, Daphne."

"I have to say though, I was so touched when I heard about

your boyfriend," Daphne said with a smirk as she made her way out of the room. "The ER nurses said he refused to leave your side. The doctors had to kick him out of the treatment room. That was so sweet."

Nate sighed. Darren. Even better. "Where is he now?"

"He stayed the entire morning until he got a call, then some woman came and dragged him away." Daphne grinned. "He said he'd be back though."

Nate watched Daphne stroll out of the room before groaning at the mess he was in.

He dug the phone out of the plastic bag. There was a message from Darren.

Sorry I had to leave, but I'll be back as soon as I can. Rest well. I'll see you soon. Love you, D.

Nate stared at the message and felt like crying again.

God… If you're listening. Please…

Please, what? The voice in his head asked.

Tears rolled from the corners of his eyes.

His heart was already broken, so why did it hurt so still?

Nate was asleep when Darren got back to the hospital. He kept his footsteps light, trying not to disturb Nate.

He pulled over a chair and sat down next to the bed. He could see the streaks of tears that dried at the corners of Nate's eyes. His heart ached for the pain he was causing Nate.

Was he wrong to love him? Was he wrong to allow himself the luxury?

He knew Nate loved him too. He could see it in his eyes,

hear it in his voice, feel it in the way Nate arch up to him as they made love. So why was Nate running away?

Darren rested his arm on the bed and pillowed his head on his arm, watching Nate sleep. He reached out and brushed the loose strands away from Nate's face, as he always did.

If he closed his eyes he could still see in his head the way Nate looked at him, his blue eyes glowing as a smile overtook his face.

A sudden stab of fear caused his chest to tighten.

He would always remember that moment.

He was this close to losing him forever. If that car had been going any faster. If that car hadn't seen Nate in time. If...

He couldn't imagine what life would be like without him.

He could deal with living the rest of his life not being able to touch or see Nate, as long as he knew that Nate was living well somewhere, but he knew his heart would die along with Nate if anything were to happen to him.

Darren held Nate's hand, rubbing softly on the back where it was bruised from the IV before bringing it close for a kiss.

Daphne was in his room again checking on things when Nate woke.

"Hey! How're you feeling?"

"Still achy, but much better. Thanks." Nate gave her a reassuring smile. He glanced at the clock. Ten in the morning.

"Oh good!" Daphne smiled back. "Your boyfriend was here last night. You were sleeping and he didn't want to wake you. I think he slept in that chair the whole night."

Nate nodded. He knew. He'd woken up briefly in the middle of the night and found Darren slumped in the chair, sound asleep, snoring softly. His heart tightened at how tired the man looked.

"The doctor will be by in a few minutes."

"Thanks, Daphne."

"Anytime."

The doctor came by and did their usual round of tests and concussion checks. He was given a clean bill of health.

"We recommend that you stay for another day because of the bad sprain though," the doctor said before he left. "You really shouldn't walk on that ankle for at least a week."

"I'll keep that in mind," Nate said.

He checked himself out of the hospital as soon as the doctor left.

"All of your bills have been paid for, Mr. de Luca," the woman handling his paperwork said. "You're good to go. Should I call you a cab?"

"Yes, please." Nate said as he signed his signature on the last form. "Oh, and if this person comes by looking for me, can you give this to him?"

Nate handed her a folded sheet of paper with "Darren Chase" written across the center.

"Sure thing," the woman smiled.

Walking awkwardly on crutches out of the hospital, Nate took a deep breath of the cold, crisp air. It was almost spring, but there was still a chill in the air.

The living room was dark, except for the set of three pod lights at the far end of the living room.

Darren sat in the dark, on the floor in front of his leather couch. He had a glass in one hand with a few fingers of Scotch in it.

His other hand held a sheet of paper. The paper was yellow and wrinkled at the edges, but the writing was still clear.

His phone rang but he ignored it, letting his voicemail pick up the call.

He sat staring at the far wall, where a large gallery wrapped black and white print hung from the wall. It was a photo of two man in each other's arms, kissing.

More precisely, it was a picture of Darren kissing Nate. Tony had snapped the picture when they were in the Hamptons for Christmas. It was a present from Tony, shipped to him directly from wherever Tony was at the time.

"Sorry this is late. I didn't get a chance to get it printed until now," Tony wrote in his email.

Of course, Tony didn't now at the time that Nate had left.

It'd been almost three years. It was mid November again, and this time of the year had been bad for Darren ever since…

The piece of paper in his hand was a note from Nate when he checked himself out against medical advice. Darren remembered almost losing it when he found out that Nate had gone missing from the hospital.

He didn't need to look at the paper to know what it said. He'd practically memorized its content.

He took a big gulp of the amber liquid.

My beloved Darren:

Please forgive me for what I am about to do. Understand that leaving you is by far the single most difficult decision I have ever had to make.

Make no mistake that I love you. I've loved you since the moment we met, and I will always love you, from the bottom of my heart.

My heart is broken for having to leave you. It isn't a decision that I have any choice in. For as long as that piece of contract exists between us, we will never be free to love each other the way we want to.

Poets said that love can move mountains, but they forget that it doesn't have the power to stand up to scrutiny and accusations.

Thank you for everything these past three months. It was the happiest three months of my life. Thank you for loving me. Thank you for showing me what it was all about, and that true love really does exist.

Don't come looking for me. Please. Just let me fade away from your life like a ripple in the water.

Have a good life, Darren. Live well, for me.

Darren tossed back the drink and let it burn a path down his throat.

When he closed his eyes, he could still see in his mind Nate walking out from the bedroom, sitting down next to him and wrapping his arms around him, before telling him to come to bed.

There were ghosts of Nate all over the apartment. He kept the things Nate left behind in the closet. He reread every book he knew Nate had read. He drove himself crazy thinking about him.

He had no idea where Nate went. Nate had moved after he left, and his phone was disconnected. He could've hired someone to find Nate, but he knew that Nate wouldn't appreciate the effort.

Putting the sheet of paper carefully on the table, he sobbed into his hands.

"Darren?" Kate knocked on the glass door of Darren's office before she walked in. "Hey, listen, Kyle and I are taking Mr. Matsumoto and his people to that new Bistro down by Ground Zero. It'd be really nice if you can come along."

"When are you guys leaving?" Darren asked without looking up.

"In about an hour," Kate said, looking at her watch. "Kyle's just finishing up with them."

"Sure. Just give me a call and I'll meet you guys in the lobby."

"Okie dokie," Kate said before she left with a sigh.

Darren couldn't help but feel apologetic towards his sister and his best friend. They were just worried about him; he understood. He'd practically turned into a workaholic, throwing everything into work after Nate left.

He sighed as he sat back in his chair and let his thoughts drift.

The Greenroom was a new spot that had just opened a few months ago. Situated close to the financial district, it was always packed full of business types enjoying a drink after a long day's work.

Darren walked into the bar area behind Kyle, Kate and one of their long time clients. Kate had called ahead for reservations so they were seated quickly. It was a Wednesday night, but it was unusually busy.

After they ordered their round of drinks, Darren excused himself to go to the washroom.

As he passed the bar, he saw someone that he thought he'd never see again.

Nate.

His hair was much shorter and he seemed to have gained some weight, but it was unmistakably him.

Darren felt thunderstruck as he stood in the middle of the bar staring at the man working behind the bar.

He could tell that Nate had recognized him by the shocked look on his face when their eyes met.

He walked over to the bar, sitting down.

"How've you been?" A million things went through Darren's head. Things he wanted to say to Nate, but he ended up with that one simple, unimpressive line.

"Good. Getting by," Nate began, but stopped himself. "You?"

"Good," Darren lied through his teeth. "Doing well."

"Oh." Nate smiled a sad little smile. "Can I get you anything?"

"No, we ordered already," Darren said, pointing to their table. "Kate and Kyle are here too. I just wanted to say 'hi'."

"And they're both well?" Nate looked down at the glass in his hands, avoiding Darren's gaze.

"They're good. Kate's expecting, eight months along, so imagine how she is usually and then multiply it by ten." Darren smiled softly, and Nate chuckled too.

"Poor Kyle then." Nate looked in Kyle's direction sympathetically.

"You have no idea," Darren said. "What about your aunt?"

"She passed a year ago. It was time." Nate shrugged. It was going to happen eventually, at least she left peacefully in her sleep.

"I'm sorry to hear that," Darren said apologetically. "So, you're working here now?"

"Yeah. Well, not exactly." Nate looked at Darren. "I'm the weekend shift manager, only moonlighting as a bartender a few nights a week. I usually don't work Wednesdays, but someone called in sick."

"Oh, good. Congratulations on the new job." Darren said. The look of longing in Nate's eyes as he looked at him was breaking his heart all over again. "Nate, listen…"

"Darren, please. I can't do this right now." Nate took a deep breath, looking away.

"I still think about you," Darren said. "Everyday."

"Darren… Please."

"I know. I'm sorry." Darren sighed. "Just… please, give me a call? My number hasn't changed."

Nate hesitated but then nodded. "I'll try."

"I gotta get back," Darren said as he took his leave. He gave Nate a "call me" sign as he left.

Nate stepped out of his shoes and tossed his bag and jacket on the floor before leaning on the wall and slid down slowly to the ground. His chest heaved as he fought the emotions rising in his chest.

Of all of the days and of all of the places in New York City, Darren had to show up at the restaurant he worked at.

The distraught look in Darren's eyes pulled at his heart, tearing at the old scars that he'd forgotten were there.

He'd never forgotten Darren. In the nearly three years since he'd left, he'd thought about the man every single moment of every single day. His heart still ached when he remembered the heartbroken look on Darren's face as Darren came chasing out the door for him.

Darren was in his dreams that night. Nate was lying in bed and Darren came to him. Nate reached up to kiss Dream-Darren and he kissed him back. The scene cut to them walking in the park, holding hands like a couple would. There was a cold breeze and Nate shivered in the wind. Darren turned and pulled Nate's scarf closer for him to block the wind. And then they were at the beach, somewhere tropical. Darren kissed him at sunset as their hair flapped in the wind and he told him he loved him…

Nate woke up with tears in his eyes.

Two week later, he was working his usual shift when John came in. He greeted his old friend.

After he'd left Darren, he'd gone to John for help. He told John about quitting his job.

"What happened?" John had asked as they sat on a bench at Pier 11. "Was it the client?"

"Well, yes, and no." The corners of Nate's mouth pulled into a self-deprecating smirk. "It was my fault, really."

"What do you mean?"

"I made a mistake I told myself never to make." Nate sighed. "I fell in love with him."

"Did he love you?" John asked.

"Yes. Probably more than I loved him." Nate sniffed, blinking his eyes to hold back the tears that threatened. He wasn't usually this emotional, but he couldn't help it when it came to thinking about Darren.

"Hey, now! You're starting to make me jealous!" John quipped, trying to lighten the mood.

Nate let out a laugh that was really a half-sob. "Sorry."

"I never wanted to leave him, you know?" Nate said quietly, pausing as he tried to put his tangled thoughts into words. "I didn't think I had a choice."

"What do you mean?"

"You know, the agency had an entire book on rules and regulations of what we can and cannot do. Me? I only had one rule that I absolutely cannot break." Nate said as he stared at the dim glow from his kitchen through the doorway of the bedroom. "I don't fall in love with my clients."

Nate turned his head to look at John. "There was this one guy, Sam, a few years back. We worked the same circles and he was such a sweet guy. He and one of his regulars, some heir of an industrial mogul, fell in love, and he decided to quit so he could be with the guy.

"That was until the guy's family found out about what Sam used to do for a living. The family called Sam a dirty gold-digging whore, and then they threatened the guy that if he didn't leave Sam, they'd cut him off and disown him." Nate smiled a sad smile. "The guy chose his family and his money over Sam."

"What happened to Sam?"

"He killed himself." Nate shook his head. "He slit his wrists in the bathroom of the apartment they shared."

"Ethan…" John looked at him with concern.

"I won't. Don't worry." Nate gave John a half smile. "But you've got to wonder: how heart broken does one have to be to take his own life? I know that he loves me, but I don't want a perpetual shadow hanging over our heads; that is no way to live. I can't possibly know that this wouldn't get used in the future as ammunition against me or Darren. And what would his family think when they find out the truth about my past?"

"You're afraid that people—or even this 'Darren' of yours—will think, somewhere down the line, that you're with him for the money, like all of his past lovers." John said. "So you're taking the easy way out, by leaving him first?"

Nate nodded. "Yeah, something like that."

"I'm going to say that you're a fool and you should've stayed with him, but then I know you won't listen." John glared at him disapprovingly. "But why did you quit your job then? I thought you needed the money."

"It was time." Nate said. "I've been considering quitting for a while now. This simply gave me the push I needed to get out while I still can."

"So what will you do now?" John asked.

"I don't know. I've got enough money set aside for my Aunt Rosie's hospice bills, but I haven't figured out what I'm going to do yet," Nate said, staring out the river. "Think I might go back to school."

"You know, if you need money just say so." John chuckled, ruffling Nate's long hair. "I don't mind helping"

"I didn't—" Nate tried to explain. He didn't look John up to borrow money. He could make do, working other jobs. More than anything, he needed someone to talk to.

"Kiddo, you know I've always liked you," John told him. "It wasn't just our business arrangement either. I liked you because of your attitude." John smiled at him. "Think of it as a friend helping out."

"But—"

"No buts, kiddo. At least you'll be paying me back, unlike either of my boys." John laughed. "Who should I make the check out to?"

Nate smiled, shaking his head. "Nathaniel. Nathaniel de Luca. But Nate's fine."

John had helped him a lot over the years. After he'd finally graduated, it was John that had introduced him to a few people, which in turn landed him the job he had right now.

For that, Nate was forever grateful.

"Hey kiddo! How've you been?" John greeted as he sat down in his usual spot at the bar.

"Same old. You know how it is." Nate grinned. "The more things change, the more they stay the same."

"Truer words." John smirked then frowned as he studied Nate's face. "You look… different. You feeling okay?"

"Of course! I'm great!" Nate snorted softly at the notion of him being *unwell.* "Your usual?"

"Yeah, thanks."

"And how about you? How does it feel to be back in the city full time?" Nate asked. John had divorced his wife of twenty-five years just last year after finally deciding that they weren't working at all. Both their kids were grown and had lives of their own, so there really wasn't a point in staying married just so they could be unhappy together. The last he heard, John was seeing someone. A male someone.

"It's fabulous. Caroline and I, well, we should've realized our problems a long time ago. We were just both too stubborn, you know? Now that I'm back, I feel like a new man." John laughed.

"I seem to remember somebody mention that they're seeing someone new?" Nate teased, wiggling his eyebrows.

"Well…" John blushed, making Nate laugh. "Yes, but that somebody doesn't have the permission to reveal the identity of said someone yet."

"Not even to an old friend?"

"We'll see. I'm trying to convince him to let me take him to dinner."

"Oh, so it was a *he*?"

"See, my mouth gets me into trouble. I've already said too

much." John did a zipper motion on his lips. "No more getting me into trouble, kiddo."

Nate laughed as he made his way to the other end of the bar to help other patrons.

That was when he saw Darren sitting in the corner, drink in hand, gazing at him.

Nate's heartbeat sped up.

Ever since Darren found out about his job at the Greenroom, the man had been coming in every night he worked, just sitting there, sipping his drinks. He'd sit for a few hours, looking towards Nate with longing in his eyes before leaving.

He'd wanted to go back to Darren, but what would he say? "Sorry, I hurt you. I still love you, so let's get back together?" Hell no.

The truth was that Nate would give anything to spend another night in that man's arms.

But none of that mattered now. Life would go on, as it always did.

By the end of his shift, Darren was already gone. John wanted to have coffee and catch up, so Nate suggested a cafe just down the street and told John to meet him out front when he got off shift.

"John!"

"You all done?" John gave him a warm smile as Nate approached him.

"Yeah." Nate pulled on his scarf. "Come on. Let's go."

Just as they were about to leave, Nate heard a familiar voice calling his name. "Nate."

He turned to find Darren standing behind them.

"Darren—"

"Who is he? Hmm?" Darren pointed at John. "What is he, your new 'boyfriend'?"

"He is just an old friend." Nate sighed. "Darren—"

"You stay away from him," Darren warned as he glared at John. "You hear me?"

"What is your problem, man?" John frowned, but before he could say more, Darren had sent him flying with a right hook. "Ow! The hell?"

"I told you to—"

"Darren!" Nate yelled, rushing to help John up. "Stop it!"

"Nate—"

"I said, stop it!" Nate made sure John was okay before he apologized. "I'm sorry, John. I've… I gotta take care of this. I'll make it up to you later."

"It's okay, kiddo. Plenty more time for coffee later." John waved it off. "But you need to stop being so stubborn and talk to him. You can't keep running away."

"I'm not—"

"Yes, you are." John ruffled his hair before pushing him in Darren's direction. "Go."

"Thanks, John." Nate watched John leave before turning towards Darren. "There, you happy? Can you please leave me alone now?"

"Nate, I'm sorry—"

"And you can be sorry somewhere else."

"No." Darren refused to budge. "Nate, we need to talk."

"Fine." Nate sighed. He never could say "no" to Darren. "Come on. My place is just a few blocks over."

Darren looked on with curiosity as Nate led him up the stairs into a small apartment on the third floor. He'd never been to Nate's old place, but he imagined that it probably wasn't too different.

Nate's place felt… homey. It was clean and tidy, but he could tell that Nate spent a lot of time there. There were bits and pieces of things that reminded him of the time Nate was at his place, practically living with him.

He shrugged of his coat and laid it over the back of the couch.

"You want anything? All I've got is beer and coke."

Darren stood and watched Nate go through his fridge. The image overlaid with the memories of Nate in his kitchen, and it was almost too much.

He rushed over and pulled Nate into his arms. Nate stiffened briefly before he relaxed, leaning his weight into Darren.

"God, I missed you," Darren muttered against the crook of Nate's neck as he buried his face into the space, breathing in the intoxicating scent he'd been missing. "I missed you so much."

He felt the moisture collect in his eyes but he didn't care. He had the one person he needed in his arms.

"You have no idea what it was like, without you there," Darren continued. "Everything feels so empty. Pointless."

He tightened his arms when he felt Nate move. "Please… Just… come back to me."

Nate moved again, this time turning in his arms. When Nate looked up at him, there were tears streaking down his face. "I missed you too. So much."

Darren brought his hands up to wipe away the tears from Nate's face with his thumb. "You know, I never stopped loving you."

"I know. Me too," Nate said before reaching up to give Darren a soft kiss. "I love you."

The kiss just wasn't enough. Darren wanted more. His craving for Nate was like the raging water behind a broken dam that came pouring out. He deepened the kiss, licking into the warm cavern of Nate's sweet mouth. Their tongues danced, caressing each other, desperate for more.

Nate pushed him backwards into the living room, then into the bedroom. They fell into bed tearing at each other's clothes. Nate straddled him, licking and lapping at his skin as he rocked against him. Darren rolled them over, gazing into Nate's beautiful blue eyes before taking his mouth again, kissing his way down Nate's body in worship.

He almost cried when he finally entered Nate's tight, hot channel, sliding home in one stroke. It was like water to a thirsty man, or rain over the desert. He could feel his heart come alive again as he plunged deeply into his lover.

Nate moved with him, writhing on the bed beneath him and calling out his name.

"I'm here, love. I'm here," Darren whispered into his ear as he grunted.

He came with a choked cry, emptying his load deep into Nate as his body froze above his lover. He could feel Nate tightening around his shaft as Nate's own orgasm over took him.

He held Nate tightly in his arms like he was never letting go as they basked in their afterglow.

"I love you," Darren whispered as he pressed butterfly kisses onto Nate's bare shoulders. "Don't ever leave me again. Please."

"I won't." Nate sniffed as he held onto Darren as tightly as he could. "Not leaving again. I love you."

Darren left at dawn. Nate lay in bed watching his lover get dressed.

"God, I don't want to go," Darren complained as he sat at the edge of the bed, looking at Nate.

"I wish you don't have to go either," Nate echoed. He smiled when Darren reached over to touch the side of his face before pressing kisses to his temple then lips.

"Hmm…" Darren growled. "You've gotta stop kissing me or I'll be late for work."

"You're the one that's kissing me," Nate pointed out with a grin.

"Sure, blame the one who's going to be late. Stop getting me into trouble, you!" Darren grinned back. "I'll see you later?"

Nate said softly, still smiling, "See you later. Love you."

"Love you too." Darren smiled brightly as he left, his eyes happy and content.

Nate watched Darren pad out of the bedroom before slumping back onto the bed.

Could he? Would he really be able to build a future with this man?

Nate buried his head into the pillows and breathed in deep. The soft sheets had taken on Darren's spicy natural scent. The man had been gone for less than five minutes and he was already missing him.

You're hopeless, Nate told himself.

He rolled out of bed, and took a hot shower before going into the kitchen to make coffee. His fingers kept wandering back to the spot on his neck where Darren had marked him last night. It felt tender and it tingled with the touch of his fingers—a stark reminder of their explosive reunion the previous night.

He didn't have to go to work until after lunch, so he ended up lounging at his place. He was reading the latest James Rollins when he heard someone knocking on his door.

He looked at the door, paused for a bit before getting up to answer. He wasn't expecting anyone.

"Kate?" Nate felt his jaw drop when he saw the eight months pregnant woman standing at his door. "What are you doing here? How did you know where I lived?"

Nate felt the slap in his face before Kate said anything at all.

"That, was for leaving," Kate said harshly before wrapping Nate into a tight hug. "And this is for coming back."

"Ow," Nate muttered as he rubbed at his cheek. "That hurt."

"Not as much as it did when you left, Nate." Kate walked past Nate into his apartment.

"I'm sorry," Nate said quietly. "I… I had to. I couldn't stay. It wouldn't have worked."

"I know," Kate said, keeping her back to him. "Darren told me everything."

"Oh." Nate blinked, not entirely sure how to process the information. "How did you know where I lived?"

"I… uh… I hired someone to compile a file on you after you left." Kate looked down at her hands. "I've known for quite some time. I just wasn't sure what to do with the information."

"You have a file on me?" Nate frowned.

"Like I said, I didn't know what to do with it. I know you didn't want to be found. I saw the note you wrote to Darren." Kate sighed. "But I couldn't bear to see Darren in pain like that."

"And you knew…" Nate hesitated over the words, "that I was an… escort?"

"I was a little shocked at first, when Darren told me." Kate shrugged. "But I can tell that you aren't like the lovers Darren has had in the past. You love *him*."

Kate stroked her swollen belly gently. "I never blamed you, Nate. I couldn't possibly imagine what you must've felt then, but I could guess. I liked you the first time I met you. Remember what I told you? I'd never seen Darren so happy before with anyone. You are special to him, which makes you special to me."

"Kate…"

"This morning was the first time I saw him smile like he meant it in almost three years, Nate." Kate turned around and there were tears in her eyes. "You know what he said to me? He said, 'He's back, Kate. He's back! I found him.' like some miracle had happened."

Nate could barely breathe as his chest tightened. He'd never meant to hurt Darren. "I never wanted to hurt him. I thought I was doing the right thing."

"I know." Kate paused, taking a deep breath to calm herself. "I would've done the same thing in your shoes. Which is why I'm still here talking to you."

She reached out to take Nate's hands into hers. "Don't ever scare us like that again. Promise me that."

Nate nodded. "I won't."

"I… uh… God damn hormones." Kate chuckled, wiping

the moisture from her eyes. "Listen, I gotta go, but you two are coming for Sunday dinner next week." And before Nate could say anything, "Nah-uh. You don't get to say *no* to the pregnant lady. Don't make me snap my fingers."

"Okay, Kate." Nate chuckled softly as he walked Kate to the door. "It is really good to see you again."

"You too." Kate kissed him on the cheek before she left.

Nate's phone vibrated in his pocket as he clocked out. It was Darren.

"Hey," Nate answered, and a soft smile crawled up his face.

"Hey," Darren said. "You all done?"

"Yeah, just getting ready to leave." Nate struggled with the phone as he pulled on his coat. "You?"

"I'm out front."

"You're what?" Nate asked, confused. He couldn't believe what he'd heard.

"I'm out front, waiting for you." Darren chuckled. "Hurry up," he said, then hung up the phone.

Nate felt his heart beat faster as he rushed out the front door, with his scarf and gloves still in his hand.

And there Darren was, standing in front of him, looking ever so handsome.

"What are you doing here?" Nate exclaimed, falling into Darren's arms.

"Couldn't wait to see you." Darren smiled, giving him a kiss. He took the scarf out of Nate's hands and wrapped the long garment around Nate's neck, making sure Nate was warm enough before he turned and hailed down a cab. "Come on."

"What? Where're we going?" Nate asked as Darren dragged him into the cab.

"You'll see."

Fifteen minutes later, the cab dropped them off in Midtown.

"Oh my god," Nate gasped when he realized where they were.

"This was our first date. Remember that?" Darren grinned as he watched Nate staring at the giant Christmas tree towering over the skating rink.

"Our first kiss." Nate looked over to Darren, his smile wide and his eyes glowing with happiness.

"Many firsts to come, my love." Darren wrapped his arm around Nate's waist, pulling his lover flush against him, kissing him. "I love you."

"I love you too."

*~ **FIN** ~*

About The Author

A barista by day and author by night, Alexis E. Skye is a hopeless romantic with a sarcastic brain. Loves traveling, cooking, and kicking back at the end of a day with a cold brew, a good book and some nice music.

You can find Alexis at:
www.AlexisESkye.com

or follow her on Twitter:
@AlexisESkye